"I really should go, Chad. I have to get up early," Dyana said.

"What time's the game?" Chad asked.

"Noon."

"That's early?"

"When you're out late it is." Dyana had turned back to him, ready to leave. "It was good seeing you," she said. "Thanks for the wine."

"My pleasure. Sure you want to leave? Considering our past, I mean."

"What?" Dyana wasn't sure she'd heard him right and she hadn't realized that he had come up behind her.

"Just what I said."

Dyana stood there a long moment. "I—Chad, I have to go."

"I was honest with you before, Dyana. Be honest with me now." Chad's voice was husky as he stood mere inches from her. It drove her crazy, his being so close and not touching her. His breath was warm on her neck, feathering across to her ear. "Do you really want to leave?"

Jan Mathews

Although she grew up on a farm in a small southern Illinois town and has lived in Chicago for over twenty-five years, Jan Mathews was born in Kentucky and still calls it home. She is a wife, mother, registered nurse, and writer—sometimes in that order. With a son who has a rock band and two other children who are involved in a variety of activities, she is always busy. If she could have one wish in life it would be forty-eight-hour days. She swears that her family, as well as every volunteer organization known to man, senses that she is a soft touch. She has been active in Scouting, athletic clubs, and in the PTA.

Jan's idea of heaven would be to spend a week in the wilderness—minus poison ivy—camping and backpacking. She would love to raft the Chattooga, see the Grand Canyon on horseback and watch Monday Night Football without being interrupted.

SECOND CHANCE AT LOVE™

JAN MATHEWS
CLASS REUNION

CLASS REUNION

First edition published December 1989

"Second Chance at Love" and the butterfly emblem are trademarks belonging to Jove Publications, Inc. The name "BERKLEY" and the "B" logo are trademarks belonging to Berkley Publishing Corporation.

Second Chance at Love books are published by
The Berkley Publishing Group
200 Madison Avenue, New York, NY 10016

Printed in the United States of America

CLASS REUNION

CHAPTER
One

THE GOOD THING about ten-year class reunions was that those classmates most likely to succeed hadn't—except for Chad—and the bad thing was facing old boyfriends when they had spent ten years becoming rich and famous while you had spent ten years becoming ten years older.

Although she couldn't actually see him, Dyana Kincaid knew the exact moment Chadwick Thomas Weber entered the posh Chicago hotel ballroom. An awed hush fell over the place, followed by animated shouts of greeting as one person after another crowded around him, all paying homage to the former king of Meadows High.

Blue and gold streamers hung from the ceiling and several hundred helium-filled balloons lined the walls. Tables had been set up around the perimeter of the room, which was illuminated only by candles and a strobe light near the dance floor, empty at the moment even though music blared from huge amplifiers on both sides of the stage. People gathered in tight little groups, laughing and talking and reminiscing. The reunion

1

committee sat at a long table near the front, greeting everyone and handing out mementos. Now they all stood up, cheering the man who had made good.

Would he even look her way? Dyana ran a hand through her short, dark hair and smoothed the sides of the black sequined dress she was wearing. The sexy number had cost her over a week's salary, but it had been worth every penny. Combined with the three-inch spike heels she had purchased for the occasion, she felt like a sultry seductress instead of an ordinary, everyday school counselor.

"Nervous?" Susan Morris whispered from beside her. Because they were close friends and lived near each other, the two women had come to the reunion together, driving in from a nearby suburb. They'd arrived a few minutes earlier and sat at a small table near the band.

Dyana shrugged, feigning a nonchalance she didn't feel. "Why would I be nervous?"

"Because the man is rich and famous and he's here, in this room, and because any woman in her right mind would swoon just looking at him. And because you used to go with him. There he is. God, he's still gorgeous, even after all these years. Why do you suppose we called him Tubbs? The man is awesome."

"Because he was fat."

"Chad was never fat—stocky, maybe, but not fat. He always had a great body."

"Not when we were kids."

Dyana and Chad had practically grown up together, attending the same school from first grade on. As children, he'd delighted in tormenting her. Sometimes it seemed as if he'd teased her all her life, pulling at her hair, leaving frogs or snakes or creepy insects in her desk, laughing at her. He had been a roly-poly then, but he had lost weight by the time they had gotten to high school. He'd gone away to camp that summer between eighth grade and freshman year and she hadn't seen him. She'd been surprised by the difference. Something else had surprised her, too, that fall they'd started high school. Not only had he slimmed down, but all of a sudden he had grown handsome—very handsome, tall, blond, and gorgeous. Broad-shouldered. Lean-hipped. The hottest guy in school.

And he'd stopped teasing her with bugs, except every once in a while, when he'd show her his pet spider.

"That's right, I forgot, you two knew each other way back when," Susan went on, craning her neck to see what was going on in the other part of the room. "Do you think he's going to come over here? He's talking to everyone."

"What's wrong with that?"

"I don't know. For some reason I expected him to ignore people. He is a star."

Dyana had ignored him—purposely. She could tell from the shouts that he was being led across the room to the table where all the guys who had played football with him at Meadows were sitting, clapping their hands in unison, waiting for him. The moment was almost like a flashback into the past, when he'd trot across the high school auditorium to the sound of cheers, the star line-backer. Only then she had been beside him, his girl, sharing him with everyone.

That is, until their senior year, when she'd broken up with him in a fit of pique and went out with his best friend, Tom Langford. Chad had reciprocated by dating Jeannie Williamson. Tom had lasted a week. Unfortunately Jeannie had lasted their entire senior year—and so had Dyana's argument with Chad.

Then they'd graduated. Before she knew it they'd both gone on to college, states apart. He'd been given a football scholarship. After his college career he was drafted by the pros. For the past six years he'd played for the Los Angeles Crusaders football team. According to newspaper accounts, he had just signed a lucrative contract for another six years. The thing that had really piqued her interest, though, making her want to see him tonight, was his reputation as a ladies' man. All over the country women threw themselves at his feet. Just a few nights ago he'd appeared on a well-known television talk show with some beautiful actress clinging to his arm.

For some crazy reason she'd wanted to compete. She smoothed her dress again, answering at last, "Frankly, I don't care what he does."

Susan gave her a skeptical glance. "Really? If you don't care, then why are you dressed like a neon sign?"

Dyana started at the remark, horrified. "Am I overdressed?" While she'd wanted to look good, she certainly didn't want to appear conspicuous.

"No, you look great." Susan had worn a silk dress, but nothing as fancy as Dyana's, and it wasn't nearly as seductive. It seemed to fit with her short-cut, streaked blond hair and tall, willowy shape. "Only it's obvious you're trying to impress someone. Don't worry," she went on at Dyana's stricken look, "it's okay to want to impress the people who thought you were a nerd most of your life. We all do it. That's the purpose of having a class reunion."

Dyana supposed that was at least partially true. It was just that she'd wanted to impress Chad—along with everyone else in the room.

Susan had turned back to the crowd. By now a wall of people had formed around Chad, all talking at once. "Did you see Jeannie greet him?" Susan asked. "She must have kissed him on the lips for a full five minutes."

"I thought she was married."

"She is, but so what? I'd kiss him, too, if I had the opportunity. You know, she's just as bouncy as ever. The quintessential cheerleader."

An odd word, *quintessential*, it seemed so onerous. "What an awful way to be remembered," Dyana remarked. "I'd hate to be compared in the same language as a Popsicle."

"Still jealous of her?"

Dyana rolled her eyes. "Please, Susan, all that was a long time ago."

"Yes, but high school rivalries are hard to die."

"Maybe." In a way Dyana did still feel the old rivalry. Although she had pretended nothing was wrong, she'd been devastated when she'd lost Chad, and particularly to Jeannie.

Susan laughed, shaking her head. "Remember how we used to stuff our bras with cotton, wanting to be as big as her?"

"How could I forget?" Dyana smiled, too, recalling their antics. They'd acted so silly. Certain Chad was dating Jeannie because of her breast size, Dyana had done everything except have silicone implants to increase the size of her bust, and she'd rejected that idea only because she couldn't find a doctor to perform the operation on her. Once she'd even tried water balloons, but one of them had burst in the middle of study hall when Tom Langford had run into her and accidentally jabbed her with a pencil. She'd been so mortified, standing there with water streaming down her chest, one side bigger than the other, and she felt embarrassed now, realizing that they probably weren't the only ones in the room who recalled the incident. "I don't believe some of the things we did."

"All in the name of being a teenager," Susan answered. "Just think, you don't have to pad your bra anymore."

Dyana's figure had finally rounded out into womanhood—full womanhood. But it seemed to have taken
forever. Mirror tiles formed the wall near their table,
and feeling silly from their conversation, she sucked in
her breath as she squared her shoulders and stuck out
her chest. "It's about time. What do you think? Am I
bigger than her?"

"Maybe just a little," a male voice said from behind
her—a very distinctive male voice, low and husky and
heart-wrenchingly familiar.

Damn! Dyana couldn't help but blush. He always
caught her at her worst. Though she wanted to disappear
into the woodwork, she spun around to greet him. He
stood there smiling at her with a silly grin, and for a
moment she was transported back in time again, to
when she'd first discovered him and they'd been so
much in love. It hurt even to think about it, such young
love, her first love.

"Hello, Tubbs," she murmured.

God, he looked so good. Susan was right: At this
moment the nickname did seem incongruous. Though
pictures of him were flashed on television or in newspapers almost daily, seeing him in person was a shock.
Gone was the chubby child and slightly stout teenage
boy she'd known and loved. In its place was a man, a
very virile, very handsome man. He was dressed in an
expensive suit that fit him perfectly, stretching evenly
across his broad shoulders. Yet he wore it casually, his
shirt unbuttoned at the neck, his tie slightly askew.

"Dyana?" he said. "It is Dyana Kincaid, isn't it? I've
been searching all over for you. You look wonderful.
It's great to see you."

Dyana didn't want to touch him, but since he took
her hands in his, she could hardly refuse to make physical contact. She felt swallowed up whole. Chad was a
big man, his hands rough and callused, as she'd remem-

bered. He'd explained to her once that a linebacker had rough hands because they got chewed up so much during play, caught between helmets or under spikes. That, however, didn't explain the little tingles she felt at his touch or the disturbing way her heart had started to pound just looking at him. She couldn't still be attracted to him, not after all these years. All the nervousness she'd felt coming here flooded back to haunt her and she could hardly speak. She pulled away. "I—thank you. How are you?"

"Fine. You?"

"Wonderful. I—you look good, too."

"That's an understatement." Susan stepped forward and cut in. "You're looking fabulous, Chad."

At six four, he towered over every man in the room. He'd always been tall, but now he had a football player's physique from head to toe. There wasn't an ounce of fat on his body. It had to be the way he worked out, for although Dyana had heard he weighed around two hundred and thirty pounds, he was all muscle and sinew and bone.

And flesh-and-blood sexy.

Despite his rugged appearance—or perhaps because of it—he literally oozed sensuality, right down to his pores. Once, when they'd watched him on television during a football game, Susan had remarked that he had the nicest-looking sweat of any man she'd ever seen.

"His tush isn't bad, either," Susan had joked, only she'd been dead serious. Chad was bent over in a three-point stance, his rear in the air, ready to fire off the line at the other team. "What buns," she'd sighed. "I swear, those tight pants should be declared illegal on television."

"Most people watch the game," Dyana had retorted dryly.

"I do." Susan had laughed when Dyana glared at her,

adding, "You watch football your way, I'll watch it mine."

"I'm no worse for wear," Chad said now. "I ache a little here and there, all these years tackling quarterbacks. Is it Sue?"

"Oh, I'm sorry—" Dyana gestured to her friend. "Chad, do you remember Susan Morris?"

"Of course. I'm sorry. I didn't recognize you, but then there are a lot of people here I didn't recognize." He held out his hand. "I hear you got married. Is your husband around? I'd like to meet him."

"I also got divorced," Susan answered, sighing and staring at her hand afterward as though she were trying to figure out how to pickle or preserve it. "You and Dyana were the only smart ones in the class."

Chad seemed puzzled. "How do you mean?"

She ended up sticking her hand in her pocket. "Neither of you fell for the marriage trap. I swear I met at least half our class in divorce court."

Chad didn't comment on the statistics. He turned to Dyana. "You didn't marry? I thought you were engaged. It was right after college. My mother told me she went to your bridal shower."

"She did," Dyana answered.

"What happened?"

"The relationship didn't work out." Actually her fiancé had broken up with her the day after her shower, saying he needed his freedom. She'd found out later that he'd had another girl, a girl with an age-old problem— she'd become pregnant. After seeing the guy a few months ago and realizing how loud and condescending he'd become, Dyana was glad now she hadn't made the mistake of marrying him. She had returned most of her gifts, but now she remembered that Chad's parents had been in the middle of moving to another suburb. The two families had lost contact. The iron Mrs. Weber had given her was still in a box in her mother's garage.

"No one else?" Chad asked curiously.

She shrugged. "I've been busy." And not interested. Most of her life she'd been kind of casual about men, except for Chad, going out whenever she wished, with whomever she wished, with few expectations. To date no one had measured up to her rather stringent standards for a man: tall, dark, handsome, sexy, and subservient. It had to be the feminist movement. She couldn't stand condescending men.

"Smart, if you ask me," Susan supplied laughingly. "The reunion committee voted to give her the old-maid award."

Chad looked pleased with that knowledge. A thousand-watt grin lit up his face. "Great. I'm getting the most eligible bachelor award. Maybe we can appear on stage together."

"Maybe." Why did *bachelor* sound nicer than *old maid*? Even spinster wasn't much better. Despite the fact that women had earned the right to vote aeons ago, there were still inequities in the male/female rationale, Dyana thought. Someone passed and patted Chad on the shoulder. He smiled at the person and shook hands, but he managed to turn back to her.

"Still as impulsive as ever, I see," he went on, picking up their conversation as though they hadn't been interrupted at all. "Who were you pretending to be when I walked over?"

Dyana flushed again, thinking of the moment he'd surprised her. Among the things she had developed in all these years was a chest, and she'd stuck it out for the world to see. "Jeannie."

"Jeannie Williamson?" He frowned. "Why?"

Susan started to speak. "We used to—"

"Believe me, it's not worth explaining," Dyana said, cutting in on her friend. "We were just acting silly."

"As I recall, you used to do that a lot in the old days."

Dyana could tell from his smile that he was teasing her, and the truth was, she had been impulsive as a kid. She'd done some crazy things as a teenager. "Over the years I've learned to temper my ways with some common sense," she answered. Pausing, she added, "Thankfully."

"Not too much common sense, I hope." His smile deepened and his eyes twinkled at her, as though he had a secret to share but wanted to savor it himself. "I happened to like the old Dyana. Dance?"

She glanced over her shoulder at the empty dance floor. Why in the world would he want to dance? "Now?"

"Why not? It's the best time. There's no crowd."

She glanced back at him, taking in his broad shoulders, the attractive features. His nose was bumpy from being broken during the past season and he had a slight scar near his right temple, the result of a collision on the football field. Although she could tell from the angry scrape on his cheek that he had just shaved, a stubble of beard darkened his features. *Because I don't want to be near you,* she thought. *Because even though we're grown-up, you were my first love. Susan's right: You're still absolutely gorgeous and I'm afraid I might tremble when you touch me, like I did when we were kids and we were in love.*

Not wise to admit. Besides, that was a ridiculous notion. She was a grown woman. An adult. She'd gotten over Chad Weber long ago.

"Sure," she agreed with a shrug. "Why not? It's a nice song."

If Dyana thought the room abuzz with excitement before, it didn't compare to the moment when he led her out on the dance floor and pulled her into his arms.

They stood for a moment as every eye in the room turned to them. Whispers rose from the corners, careless murmurs she could hear. "Look, he's with Dyana Kincaid. Remember when they used to date? What in the world did he see in her?" from the women to "Wow!" from the men. "That's Dyana Kincaid. Has she changed!"

She tossed her head back and smiled. Who was she fooling? The only reason she had dressed to the nines, slinking around in an expensive sequined dress and towering on three-inch spike heels was in the hope that he'd notice her. Now she had her wish. If only his touch weren't so disturbing. His hand felt like a hot poker on her back as he folded her into his arms and moved her along in time to the music, a nice slow waltz. The strobe light reflected on her dress, flashing prisms on his face, casting it in light and shadow.

"So," he said, twirling her around the dance floor, "let's play catch-up. Tell me about Dyana Kincaid."

"What about Dyana Kincaid?"

"What have you been doing all these years?"

She gave an offhand shrug. "Nothing special. I'm a high school counselor."

Another revelation that seemed to surprise him. He glanced at her with a startled expression. "You, a high school counselor? You were always in trouble."

She laughed, agreeing. She had spent more time in her counselor's office than in the classroom. She wasn't a bad student, exactly, just impulsive and prone to pulling pranks. "Maybe that's why I chose it for a profession. I felt comfortable there."

"That's a good point." He frowned at her in a slow, disturbing assessment. "I'll bet you're good at it. Do you like kids?"

"Does anyone like kids, particularly teenagers?" she

returned. "I do have an understanding of how kids can think, though. And act."

"Still pull pranks?"

"Sometimes," she admitted.

"Right down to conspiracy?"

She smiled. "I've been known to lead a student movement or two."

Her confession made him chuckle. "I knew it. So tell me about your ill-fated engagement. What happened?"

The man was puzzling; he was certainly curious. "What is this, twenty questions?"

"We've got a lot to catch up on. I haven't seen you in ten years. Did you break up with him?"

"No, he broke up with me."

"Why?"

Dyana frowned. Probing was probably a more appropriate term, but he was getting downright nosy. "The usual," she said. "He met someone else." Her frown deepened. Come to think of it, she had a big chest, too.

"The usual? How many fiancés have you lost?"

Dyana shook her head, not willing to admit she'd been referring to him. While she had broken up with him all those years ago, when she'd wanted to get back together, he'd stayed with Jeannie Williamson, which had irritated her. No, *irritated* wasn't quite the correct word. It had hurt her when he'd stayed with Jeannie, deeply. "Only one fiancé," she said. "but I have bad luck with men."

"Is that so? Well, cheer up. Luck is easy to change."

"Really? How?"

"Just by being here."

"I don't think I follow."

"You're dancing with me, aren't you?"

His conceit was as bad as his curiosity. "No problems with your ego, I see."

"None at all." When she gave him a haughty arch of

her eyebrow, he laughed and twirled her across the dance floor again. But he wasn't done talking. They'd barely finished that conversation when he asked, "How's your family? Did your sister ever have all those kids she talked about?"

Dyana nodded. "Everyone's fine. Despite my protests and extreme embarrassment at fifteen, I ended up the happy aunt of three darling children."

"Is Darcy still married to that guy you slugged with the gin bottle? What was his name, Phillip?"

"Yes. Phillip Manning. They're very happy."

"He never sued you?"

"No, thank goodness." It had been a horrible moment. Because of a dating-service application Dyana had filled out—or rather *mis*filled out when she'd been angry at her sister—Phillip had come to the house thinking Dyana's older sister a prostitute and wanting to interview her for a study he was doing. Certain the "professor" had ulterior motives, Dyana had hit him over the head with a gin bottle. "But that's probably because he's in love with Darcy."

"A nice love?"

"I hope so. I like to think it's a forever love."

"That's the best kind."

"Yes," she agreed.

Perhaps it was the inflection in her voice, for he glanced at her with a quizzical expression. "Something wrong?"

Even though they'd been kids, she'd thought her love for him a forever love. They'd broken up over a remark she'd made about a rock. *A rock, for God's sake.* They'd argued about the silliest things. Then she'd crushed his pet spider, accidentally, of course, when she'd slammed the piece of quartz down on his dresser. "No, nothing's wrong." She took a deep breath, pushing away the memories. "So why didn't you ever marry?"

she asked, telling herself she wanted to keep up the conversation. Odd, though, how her breath caught in her throat, waiting for his answer.

"I never found anybody as fun-loving as you."

"Right." She leaned back in his arms so that she could see his face. "You talk quite a line these days, Chad. I can see why women flock after you."

"Women flock after me for no other reason than because I'm a celebrity," he answered, drawing her close again. "But you wound me, Dyana. I wasn't giving you a line."

"Sure, and the moon's made of green cheese."

"Are you saying you don't believe me?"

"Please, Chad, don't play dumb. It doesn't become you."

He chuckled deep in his throat. The sound rumbled through his chest lazily, like distant thunder on a summer night. "Still the same old Dyana, aren't you? Honest and outspoken. Okay, no line. Truthfully, though, the only reason I came here tonight was because I had hoped to see you."

She studied him a long moment, trying to assess the truth of his statement. If he was being honest, she should be flattered. "Really?"

"Really. However, I did think you were married. That's why I never tried to contact you all these years."

"So you were safe?"

"Tonight? Asking you to dance?" He flashed another grin. "Yes, so to speak, but I'm not safe anymore, and I'm still dancing with you."

She still couldn't decide whether or not to believe him. Finally she shrugged and said, "I had hoped to see you, too."

He glanced at her dress pointedly. "So I gathered."

No doubt about it, the man's ego was gargantuan. Pretty soon he'd need a tractor trailer to haul it around in. "You really are suave, aren't you, Chad? All the answers."

Surprisingly his response was serious. "I'm not a teenage kid anymore," he said in a low, somber tone. "But no, I don't have all the answers. I wish I did."

So did Dyana, for although the music ended, he didn't let her go. Several people passed by, patting him on the shoulder, congratulating him on one feat or another. It amazed her how he could smile and acknowledge them and still pay total attention to her. His clear blue eyes were riveted to hers, and while he wasn't holding her close at all, she was vividly aware of every inch of him, like lightning shattering her soul. What in the world was happening to her? She felt as though she'd been on a roller-coaster ride, dipping and swaying and losing her heart, and all she'd done was dance with him.

She didn't move away. When the band started to play another song, he took her back into his arms. This time the tune was an old one, low and throbbing with sensuality, the movements a cross between a mambo and making love, all hip action. Dyana didn't think Chad would know it, but he held her stiffly and dipped her backward from the waist. Slowly. Down. Then, in one quick, smooth movement, he pulled her up against him, staring into her face as they paused for a heartbeat.

Dyana was spellbound as he began the complicated steps, pulling her close, pushing her away. Dipping. Swaying. "You're a very good dancer," she said after a moment. It made her wonder what else he did well.

"So are you."

"But you're a football player."

"Does that make me uncoordinated?"

Dyana flushed. "No, of course not. I'm sorry. I didn't mean it that way. I was just surprised. You never danced when we dated."

"I was too busy trying to act cool."

The dance they were doing was certainly hot, slow and sultry and seductive. She wished the band would come up with something fast, a square dance or a polka. A minuet, even. Chad kept staring down into her face, not touching her yet making her aware of him. Teasing. Dipping. Swaying. He was so close to her that she could feel the heat from his body, the living, breathing flesh, and he was so damn sexy, it was a crime. The smell of his after-shave assailed her nostrils, along with an inherent maleness that was his and his alone. But it was the distance between them that made the moment—and the movements seem so beguiling. Trying to concentrate on something other than their bodies, which were practically touching, she willed her feet to follow his steps.

All of a sudden he stopped dancing and stood stark still with his arms around her, her body still near his. Surprised by his abrupt pause, she murmured breathlessly, "We made some dumb mistakes, didn't we?"

"Yes," he agreed, reaching to caress her cheek. Once again she stood immobile. Actually she couldn't move away. She felt riveted to the spot as he drew his hand slowly along her jaw, to her chin, up to touch her lips and linger. "My biggest mistake was in not apologizing to you for our argument."

"You thought you were right."

He flashed his grin again, that lopsided quirk of his mouth that drove women wild. She had followed his career, and once, during an interview, a female sportscaster had sighed out loud when he'd smiled. Now Dyana wanted to do the same thing. Actually, what she really wanted to do was close the distance between them and let him kiss her.

"I still do think I was right," he answered. "Only

these days I know enough to say I'm sorry, anyhow, right or wrong."

"I killed your spider."

"I survived."

At the time he hadn't felt so generous. "Style, grace, diplomacy. Brute strength. My, you've come a long way, Mr. Weber."

"I hope so."

Too far for her. She was way out of her league. Why in the world had she come here tonight? Why had she danced with him? This wasn't a kid she was playing with, her Tubbs, even though he was an old flame. This was fire. Smoldering embers waiting to explode into a raging inferno. Being with him was like dumping gasoline in a forest and then tossing a match. Carelessly.

Tempting fate.

"Excuse me," she said, needing to get away. The things he could do to her with a mere touch were upsetting. Her skin felt flushed, as though she had a fever, and her insides were shaking like dry leaves on a windy day.

But Chad pulled her back into his arms. "What's wrong?"

She took a deep breath, trying to get her bearings. "I think dinner's being served."

He glanced around. The song had ended, and those few people that had accompanied them on the dance floor were leaving to sit at the tables. One of their classmates went to the microphone. Most everyone else stood watching them. "Yes, I believe you're right. May I join you?"

"I'm sitting with Susan."

"No extra chairs?"

She paused. "Chad, why are you doing this?"

"What?"

"Pursuing me."

He laughed again and frowned at her. "Pursuing you?"

"Coming on to me, then," she said, amending the term.

"What makes you think I'm coming on to you?"

"Why else would you sit with me?" *Why would you dance with me like that?*

"Because you're a good conversationalist?" When she shook her head at his answer, he said, "Then how about for old times' sake? No? Okay. Would you believe because we're both single and we used to go out together?"

"No."

"Dyana, I told you before, the only reason I came here was to see you."

"Sorry" she said, "I didn't believe you then, and I certainly don't believe you now."

"I know. It's such a shame. You have a problem with the moon. Those poor little mice have been busy all these years making holes, and you don't appreciate them at all."

If only his voice weren't so low and husky and sincere. Dyana studied him a long moment. It was hard to tell if he was making fun of her or not. While he was obviously joking, his expression had remained dead serious. What could he possibly see in her? Chad Weber, sports hero and legend, and Dyana Kincaid, everyday girl. Never mind that he used to be her knight in shining armor. They were like Superman and Lois Lane. Romeo and Juliet.

Antony and Cleopatra.

"All right." She turned away and headed toward her table. Although she still didn't believe him, she motioned to a chair. What was one dinner sitting beside him—a reunion dinner at that? This was what she'd wanted, for him to notice her. Just because he had a reputation as a ladies' man didn't mean he would sweep her off her feet like he had when they were teenagers. But as more whispers followed them from the dance floor she began to wonder. The boy she had known as Tubbs had not only grown into a virile, handsome man, but also he was dangerously charming, and her feet were already feeling a tad like Dorothy's in *The Wizard of Oz*, served by a click and a wish.

When they got back to the table, Susan was sitting with a group of women who had congregated, former classmates, all waiting to giggle and flirt with Chad. Susan had given Dyana a high sign of approval for their dance, but from the way everyone acted, Dyana might not have been present during the two songs. Chad was hailed as the next Fred Astaire or, better yet, the new Patrick Swayze. The subject went from dancing to football to outright idiocy. It seemed that the only thing he couldn't do was walk on water. But surely that would be next. They could all prostrate themselves on the ground in adoration as he parted the Red Sea or multiplied the fishes and loaves. Chad didn't seem to mind being the center of attention. Then again, he was accustomed to women fawning over him. After dinner, when they gave him the Most Eligible Bachelor award, he waded through the gaggle of well-wishers, laughing and hugging and letting them kiss him on the cheek or touch his hand and sigh.

"You're next," he murmured to her.

"How thrilling."

"I don't think you're into this, Dyana."

"I'm not." But when her name was called, she walked forward gamely. This *was* a class reunion.

The man who had been their class president hadn't changed much in ten years. When it came to the opposite sex, he was shy, and most of the time they'd been growing up, he'd had a ridiculous expression on his face. Glancing at him now could have been another moment suspended in time, which was probably why Dyana had the sudden impulse to do something outrageous. That and the fact that Chad was watching her.

"Here we go, *Miss* Dyana Kincaid," the guy said with a flourish, handing her the trophy. "The Old Maid of Meadows High."

"Thank you." She smiled graciously and glanced down at the award. If she'd been any more dramatic, they might have given her the Academy Award. In fact, she couldn't have done better had she been an actress. "There are a lot of people I must thank for this honor," she started to say when the applause died down. "First my mother and my father. And, of course, my sister and my brother—"

"What are you talking about, Dyana?" Susan stage-whispered from the sidelines. "Why are you giving this speech? You don't have a brother."

"I don't?" Dyana pretended to be confused, frowning at the trophy. "Then my friends. And certainly my dog and cat."

Susan was coming positively unglued. She leaned forward, a worried expression on her face. "Dyana, what in the world are you pulling?"

Dyana just smiled. "And, of course, Jeannie Williamson and Chad Weber." A chuckle broke out here and there as people realized what she was getting at. "And flat chests." Which brought down the house. "Thank you all, particularly Mother Nature." With that she stood sideways, squared her shoulders again, and winked. "Eat your heart out, guys."

The crowd roared, laughing and clapping. But Dyana wasn't done yet. She should have known better than to involve Chad, particularly after their dance, but she was still feeling mischievous and she crooked her finger at him. He bounded up on stage as though he'd been waiting for her signal. "You know," she told him when he stood beside her, "this is all your fault."

Even his frown was sexy. "Why's that?"

"You accused me of not being into this. Let's really shock them." She turned to the microphone. "And now, former classmates, what you've been waiting for, the Old Maid of Meadows High and the Most Eligible Bachelor will provide the evening's entertainment. For old times' sake."

"Dyana, are you all right?" Chad asked as she turned to him.

"I'm fine."

"Then will you please tell me what the hell's going on?"

"What else?" She puckered her lips. "Kiss me, Mr. Weber."

"Kiss you?"

"You do know how?"

Her second mistake. She shouldn't have challenged him. With a mocking arch of his eyebrow he answered, "Oh, yes, I know how. You're sure you want me to kiss you?"

"Absolutely."

"All right," he said, gathering her tightly against his hard length. "My pleasure, Miss Kincaid. One kiss coming up. For old times' sake."

Although she'd asked for it, Dyana was unprepared for the depth of his embrace. Didn't he realize they were onstage, with everyone watching? They were supposed to be pretending, acting silly, but there was nothing silly about the way he held her, pressed shamefully to his body, or how his lips met hers, hot and hard and demanding. How they felt, so rough and yet at the same time soft. Provocative. Fire blazed through her, red-hot and sizzling, leaping, soaring flames. She gave a little utterance of protest, but he gathered her closer, kissing her for so long that she thought she might faint.

"Goodness" was all she could murmur when he let her up for air.

"More! More!" the crowd chanted, but Dyana didn't hear them. Her pulse was roaring and pounding in her ears.

"Ready?" he whispered huskily.

"For what?" Thank goodness he was holding her. She was still a bit breathless. How could he affect her this way? Her knees were shaking and her legs felt weak and her heart was hammering so fast, she felt certain she was in danger of cardiac arrest.

"The finale. It's time to carry you away. I'll toss you over my shoulder and cart you out the door. They'll love it."

"Where will we go?"

"Again" from the crowd. "Kiss her again, Chad!"

"I don't know. We'll find somewhere. I could always give you a lift home."

"I came with Susan."

"Does she have a ride home?"

Dyana nodded. "Yes, she drove."

"Will she mind if you leave?"

"I don't know. I didn't ask her."

Chad smiled. "That settles it, then. Hang on."

"Wait." Dyana hesitated, not quite certain she wanted to go that far. A joke was one thing, going home with a man another, even if that man was a former classmate and high school sweetheart. Even if she'd practically grown up with him. Even if he was Tubbs. Besides, he had just kissed her, quite thoroughly and passionately. "I'm not sure we should just leave."

"Why not? We deserve a great exit."

"What about all the people?"

"I suppose we could stay and chat with Jeannie Williamson and Tom Langford and all the other curiosity seekers who don't really give a damn about us."

Put that way it seemed as though Dyana had little choice—given the premise that she *wanted* a choice. She glanced at the crowd of people still gathered around the stage, laughing and clapping for them, thinking they were putting on a show. Well, hadn't they? She glanced at Chad, at the appealing smile on his face. The man was awesome. Tall and handsome. Charming. Sexy as all get-out. A professional football player who was rich and famous and who was standing there waiting for her to leave with him. In the name of gossip, of course. She, Dyana Kincaid, girl wonder. She had to be daft to turn him down. On the other hand, there was the wind that buffeted her feet. A tricky wind. The last thing she needed was to fall in love. Again. With him.

"Dyana?"

The decision was made for her when she happened to notice Tom Langford maneuvering his way through the crowd, a grin on his face and a pencil in his hand, Jeannie Williamson at his side. Dyana turned back to Chad and slipped her arms around his neck. "Let's go, Lancelot. I'm all yours."

"Lancelot?"

Obviously he wouldn't understand. "I could have called you Clyde, as in Bonnie and Clyde."

Which made him laugh. "Am I that dangerous?"

"Yes."

"I promise to take good care of you."

"That's what I'm afraid of."

"I see." With another deep chuckle he scooped her into his arms and started across the stage. "In that case, you'd better hang on, Guinevere, because my horse is right outside and we're going to go for one hell of a ride."

His statement did little to set her mind at ease. "Only for the moment," she said, qualifying it.

He just laughed. Then he winked at her and mur-mured huskily, "Being that you're the class spinster, this may come as a surprise to you, Miss Kincaid, but when it comes to men, there are some things a girl really shouldn't count on."

CHAPTER
Two

TO THE DELIGHT of their classmates, Chad carried
Dyana off the stage, across the ballroom, into and
through the hotel lobby, onto the sidewalk, and to his
car. Before scooping her in his arms, he'd handed her
their trophies, and she held them, one in each hand, as
almost everyone followed behind, Pied Piper-like, circling in a long line around the potted plants and fancy
furniture adorning the lobby, and spilling out onto the
street to cheer and shout. In any other city in the world
the group would have been ignored, but this was Chicago, the conservative Midwest, and people stopped
what they were doing or where they were going on the
soft, balmy night to turn and stare, smile and laugh, no
doubt thinking Dyana was a newlywed being carted off
by her groom.

Since the assemblage was basically a friendly sort,
Dyana managed to ignore everyone—whistles, catcalls,
and all—concentrating instead on how she was going to
handle Chad. His remark had totally unnerved her. No,
he totally unnerved her. The man who was helping her
play a practical joke on the alumni of Meadows High

was more than she had bargained for, and she didn't
know how she was going to keep from going with him.

He hadn't been exaggerating. His horse was right
outside, only it wasn't a great white stallion like Lancelot would ride. A bright red Mercedes convertible with a
vanity license plate that read WEBER 99 sat parked at the
curb. In addition to his name, which was as well known
as the president's, or perhaps more so, the number was
the same as his football jersey.

"Should we give them one more thing to talk about?"
he asked, still holding her in his arms.

She hadn't been paying attention to him; she'd been
busy thinking, contemplating escape. "Talk about?
What do you mean?"

"This." Abruptly he kissed her again, dropping the
hand that held her legs so that at the same time their lips
met, she slid down his body in a slow, sensuous movement. Dyana couldn't help it, she felt weak inside, all
shaky and out of breath. When he let her go she practically fell into the car seat. She had no choice but to
leave with him. That or run. Which wasn't an option at
all. She was incapable of making her legs move or her
lungs breathe deeply enough to function. All she could
do was hold onto the trophies. And even if she could
run, she could see herself explaining why she had
sprinted off down Michigan Avenue, fleeing from her
class reunion.

But, officer, he kissed me in front of my classmates.

In spite of the fact that the Mercedes didn't have tin
cans tied to the bumper, their send-off was sensational.
The crowd surged around the car, still laughing and
cheering as Chad got in on his side and started the engine.

"Hang on," he said, "we're off and galloping."

With that he pressed on the accelerator. The car
surged out into the street like a shot from a cannon, only

smooth, even, powerful. Behind them there were shouts of encouragement. Since the top was down, wind whipped through her hair, playing havoc with the short tresses.

After merging with the traffic, Chad slowed down and glanced at her. "We made it."

"Yes." Still trembling from her reaction to him, she ran her fingers through her hair, straightening the strands.

"Well, what do you think?"

She glanced at him. "About your kissing me?"

"No," he said. "About the car."

"Oh." She glanced at the Mercedes. "Yes, the car." She ran a hand over the plush upholstery, almost afraid of marring it. She couldn't even afford insurance on an automobile like this. "It's very nice. Did you have a choice of color?"

He smiled. "Don't you like red?"

"It's so typically macho."

"And I'm not?"

Now she was the one who smiled. There ought to be a law against it: Even though he was macho, he was charming. "You are."

"You've really got a bad impression of me, Dyana," he said. "I can see I'm going to have to work hard to correct that."

"Why would you want to correct it?"

"Because I don't like people thinking badly about me."

"Then you shouldn't drive a red Mercedes."

"It was given to me for being chosen MVP of the Super Bowl last January. I couldn't turn it down. That would have been impolite."

She frowned. "I thought it was a Lamborghini." She had watched the game and she'd been amazed at how the car doors opened when they'd presented it to him, lifting up in the air like giant wings. She'd wondered what would happen if the battery ever went dead. How would he get in the car? Or out of it?

"No, the Lamborghini was for being MVP of the Pro Bowl," he explained. "I gave it to my folks. My dad gets a real kick out of it."

Dyana could well imagine. She remembered Mr. Weber, Senior, as a quiet man, house-slippered and pipe-smoking yet with a devilish glint to his eyes. He would enjoy something wild. "You've done well with your career, Chad."

"I work hard."

Oddly, as egotistical as he'd seemed before, there was nothing smug about the way he answered now. And he did work very hard. He had a reputation for giving his all and more on the football field. She ran a hand over the seat of the car again. "It's really quite impressive. I'm amazed it's intact, though, considering where you parked." As far as she was concerned, no one in their right mind would leave an expensive car on the street in a major city.

"Actually, so am I," Chad answered. "I paid a kid fifty bucks to watch it, but I didn't see him when we came out. He must have skipped as soon as I gave him the cash."

"You paid someone to watch your car and actually expected the person to stick around?"

He smiled. "I'm naïve."

"Oh, sure."

"Okay, I confess. I didn't want to park it in a garage. I used to work in one, and all the attendants drive like maniacs."

"I see."

He must have sensed her skepticism. He glanced at her. "Have you ever parked in one of those places?"

She laughed. "I park in them all the time. Only I drive a Ford Fiesta."

He laughed along with her. "Point taken."

"Where are we going?" she asked after a moment. Their conversation had relaxed her a bit, but she still had some qualms about being with him. What if he kissed her again? Hell, he didn't have to kiss her. All he had to do was touch her, look at her, and she wanted to melt in his arms. She had to do something to shore up her defenses. It wasn't wise sitting beside him feeling vulnerable.

"I thought we'd go to my place and visit awhile," he answered. "Do you mind?"

"Oh." How surprising. "No." How nice. It was almost a pleasant prospect. After all these years she would enjoy visiting with his folks. She'd always liked them. She could apologize for not returning the iron. "That sounds like fun."

"Good. Then we're off."

Chad had turned onto the boulevard that ribboned the Chicago lakefront from the south side of the city to the north. Lake Michigan was to their right, the city on their left. Hundreds of brightly lit buildings formed the skyline, which seemed to rise up, phoenixlike, almost from the water's edge. All that separated the tall buildings in the downtown area from the lake was the road and a park and lots and lots of sky. One of the nicest things about the city was its feeling of spaciousness, even in the downtown area.

The wind still whipped through her hair, but Dyana relaxed against the car seat, knowing they had a distance to go. A few seconds later, she sat forward again, confused when he turned off the road. "Did your parents move again?"

He'd headed down the short street leading to one of the high-rise buildings just north of the Loop. The buildings had all been constructed right on the lake-shore, nearly jutting out over the water. This one was one of Chicago's most exclusive and expensive, with a distinctive curved shape, almost like a rounded triangle. A bubble-covered pool on the lower floor that faced the Outer Drive added to its appeal. The rich and luxurious could parade around in bathing suits all year long.

"No. They still live in Winnetka." Chad's expression was puzzled. "Why?"

"I thought we were going there." All her trepidations were beginning to return. She couldn't be alone with him. Not in an apartment—his apartment!

"To my folks' house?" He still seemed puzzled. "Why?"

"I thought you lived with them." Actually he lived in Los Angeles, where he played football. Dyana knew that, but she'd assumed that while he was in town he would stay with his parents.

"Don't you think I'm a little old to be bunking in with my family?"

"No."

By then he had pulled into the private parking lot, which was a part of the building, sprawling underneath like a giant catacomb. He nestled the car into a numbered parking space. "Are you still living with your folks?"

"No," she said again, "but I live here, in Chicago. You're visiting."

"I still value my privacy."

"So you rent an apartment for when you're in town?"

"Yes."

She could tell that didn't seem odd to him. "What about when you're not here? Isn't the apartment kind of expensive to maintain?"

"Actually it's a good tax deduction," he said. "Besides, my folks use it. So do friends. Believe me, it

doesn't sit empty. Is something wrong, Dyana? Are you
having second thoughts? Do you mind coming up?"

Was the earth round? The universe vast? Loving
Marc Antony the cause of Cleopatra's demise?

"No, of course not," she lied, knowing she'd feel
silly if he suspected the truth. She was twenty-seven
years old, hardly a shrinking violet. She'd been in a
man's apartment before. *But not this man's apartment.*

"Good." He opened his door and go out, coming
around to help her from the car. "I wouldn't want you to
feel uncomfortable."

"Gee, thanks," she murmured under her breath.

"Excuse me?"

"Never mind." She could do this. She was going to
be fine. But as she glanced at the elevator in the distance, it looked more like a trap than a vehicle of conve-
nience. She'd always had a vivid imagination, and all of
a sudden the doors twisted open, turning into steel-
jawed teeth, waiting to snap closed on the unsuspecting
girl quarry.

She blinked the vision away. One of these days she
was going to try writing and drawing cartoons. Or horror novels. She already knew the first line: Elvis is alive
and well and living in Ohio next door to James Dean.

"Something wrong?" Chad asked.

"No. I'm just—I've never been here before." Dyana
had been juggling their trophies, trying to get a hold of
them and smooth her dress at the same time. Whenever
she sat down, the sequins itched.

Taking the trophies from her hands, Chad steered her
toward the yawning chasm. "It's a nice building. Good
security." They passed a guard, who nodded and waved
them on. Ironically the man looked like a conductor.
Then there was Tubbs, the hero at her side.

"Dyana?"

"What?"

"Are you coming?"

She'd paused at the elevator entrance, and now she stepped forward. "Something was wrong with my shoe."

"Is it okay?"

"Fine."

"The view isn't great"—he went on talking about his apartment as he escorted her off of the elevator and down the hall toward his door, number nine on the second floor—"but it isn't awful, either. I didn't think about it until after I had already moved in—the upper floors are nicer. There's also less traffic noise."

"Cars?"

He nodded. "Day and night, from the Outer Drive and the parking lot. Delivery vans."

Actually the view was breathtaking. When he opened the door, Dyana just stood there and stared, amazed. They weren't that high up, but one whole wall of the apartment was windows, and the expanse of Lake Michigan seemed to go on forever. Although it was late at night, the moon hung low over the lake, illuminating the area with a soft glow. Lights flickered in the darkness, boats moved up and down the shore. An occasional beam shot through the fog that shrouded the surface of the water like a hovering mother. In the distance she could make out a lighthouse and the promontory.

"It's beautiful," she murmured.

He gave the scene a cursory glance as he went around clicking on lamps. "You should see it during a storm. Come on in, make yourself at home."

She glanced around the apartment as she stepped inside and closed the door behind her. In addition to this room, a kitchen arched off to one side, and what was obviously a hall leading to a bedroom on the other. Everything was beautifully done, elegant, from the stark white walls and carpet to the pale pink sofa and chairs that formed a conversation pit. The furniture was silk, hardly what she'd expected of Chad, yet suitable somehow, since it was so big, massive. Although feminine in color, everything was masculine in style. Splashes of color provided contrast, an amethyst rock, a gilt-framed painting, fluffy throw pillows in purple, pink, and green. One entire wall was mirrored, not with tiles but with a full-length floor-to-ceiling wall-to-wall mirror reflecting all the accents. Combined with the view and the expanse of windows, the effect was stunning.

"This is gorgeous," Dyana remarked. "Did you do the decorating?"

"Most of it. I was lucky to sublet from a guy named Angus Behr, and he recommended a decorator to help with the finishing touches. She picked out the pillows and stuff." As he spoke, Chad took off his suit coat and tie and tossed them over a dining room chair. The table was glass, too, sitting up on a raised platform. Getting comfortable, he unbuttoned his shirt collar and sleeves, rolling them to this elbows. "Since I'm here so seldom, I didn't want to have a lot to clean."

It would be easy to clean. Very little cluttered the glass-topped tables: more rocks, a photo, a potted plant. "Odd name, Angus Behr."

Chad nodded agreement. "I'm sure he gets some flak on it. Nice guy. Hated giving up the place, although he was really delighted to be getting married. His wife-to-be's name was Hillary Lambert—not very common, either." He gestured to the sofa. "Have a seat. Kick off your shoes if you want. Those heels look uncomfortable. Maybe that's why you tripped earlier."

"I think I tripped on a grating."

"They still look uncomfortable. Feel free to go barefoot. I'll get us something to drink. Do you like wine? I think I have some Chablis in the refrigerator."

"Chablis sounds great."

While he disappeared into the kitchen, Dyana sat down on the sofa. She really should make an excuse to leave. She was living dangerously sitting here. And she certainly wasn't going to take off her shoes.

Don't be silly, Dyana, she told herself. He hasn't done anything except chat. Even in the elevator he'd hardly touched her. But, oh, what a touch. She'd held herself stiffly erect, ignoring the strong fingers pressing into her back, the tendrils of awareness traversing her spine.

"Here we go." He came back into the room with two long-stemmed glasses of wine, handing her one. Tipping his glass to her, he said, "Cheers."

She lifted her glass to her lips. "Yes, cheers."

Thankfully he took a chair across from her. Still she was aware of him, the incredible body, his eyes on her. It was silly, but she was growing increasingly anxious. What would happen now? She felt like a teenager, wondering what the first move would be and petrified of it.

Chad didn't seem in the least nervous. He placed his glass on the table. "Taste all right?"

"Fine," she murmured. "It's great."

"Good. Glad you like it."

He said that a lot, she noticed, *good*. It made her uneasy. *Good* was used to reward little children who didn't misbehave, to compliment a host on dinner, or to acknowledge chaste women. And the way he was staring at her was not the way a man looked at a chaste woman.

Purposely glancing away, she took another sip of wine. "It's nice."

"The wine?"

"Yes."

"It's just Chablis."

"But it's really nice." She was making a fool of herself and he hadn't done a thing.

"Good," he answered.

She smiled brightly. Clearly another tack was needed. "So," she murmured, draining the glass and placing it on the table, "what have you been doing all these years?"

He watched her drink the wine with a look of concern on his face. But he didn't remark. "Me?"

"Yes." The question had been silly, too, but she could hardly back down.

"Playing football."

"Do you like it?" She kept topping herself, getting stupider and stupider.

"Football?"

"Some people don't like their jobs, Chad."

"That's true," he agreed, looking at her with that silly expression of his. No doubt about it, the man was as sexy as all get-out. "But I happen to love football. How about you? Ever watch a game?"

"Sometimes." It wasn't a lie, exactly. She only watched the games he played in. She picked up her wineglass, surprised that it was empty.

"Would you like more?"

"No, I've had plenty." She'd practically guzzled the stuff. She had to get hold of herself. Next she'd be getting tipsy. In fact, she was already feeling a bit dizzy. Amazing how a single drink could do her in.

"Sure?"

"Yes. I can't stay long, anyhow. I have a soccer game in the morning."

"You play soccer?"

"Hardly. I know nothing about the game. Darcy's kids play," she told him. "I just cheer them along."

"You know, Dyana, to a person who likes football, soccer's a bad word."

"Do you like football?" It wasn't until the words were out of her mouth that she realized she'd asked them before.

Chad just grinned at her. "You seem awfully nervous."

"I am."

"Why? I won't hurt you."

She studied him for a long moment. "Not intentionally, maybe."

"Not even unintentionally," he said.

"I haven't seen you in over ten years, Chad."

His glance was as serious as hers had been. "That's also true, but I can assure you that I haven't become an ax murderer in that time. Why are you so uncomfortable with me?"

She wished she could answer. One thing she knew, she was behaving ridiculously. Even a teenager acted more mature. All he'd done was kiss her. Twice. "I don't know. You scare me," she said at last. "I—you're famous."

"I'm the same guy you knew in high school."

The same guy who had teased and cajoled her. And kissed her and made her fall in love with him. "Not really. You're different. I'm different."

"I suppose in a way we're both different," he agreed. "We're grown-up."

Which was what frightened her more than anything. Although they were grown-up and she hadn't seen him for over ten years, she still wanted him. She'd been with him for all of two hours and she wanted him. She knew it was wrong—totally, ridiculously, ludicrously, stupidly wrong—and still she wanted him. What she wanted was for him to kiss her like he had when they'd dated, like he had before he'd gone out with Jeannie Williamson.

And because of what she wanted, what she needed was a good shrink.

Pusing herself up from the sofa, she went to glance out the window at the lake, thinking the activity might help her regain her perspective. The water was dark, deep, dotted with small white boats. "What's it like during a storm?"

"Incredible. A little frightening because you don't have control, particularly the squalls that come up quickly."

An interesting description. She turned back to him. "Did you get good grades in college, Chad?"

He must have been puzzled by her abrupt change in attitude. He stared at her for what seemed forever. Actually she was surprised by her attitude, too. She should leave, take her purse and her trophy, and catch a cab home. Instead she waited for him to answer.

"Mostly."

"I almost failed."

"You went to a tough college," he remarked. "I always wondered why you chose a private university."

She was surprised that he knew where she'd gone. She didn't think he'd kept track of her. She sat back down across from him. "My sister wanted me to go somewhere small so I wouldn't get caught up in the social life."

"But you did, anyhow?"

"Of course. Don't we all? There just seems to be more to do at a big university." She started to pick up her wineglass again but stopped.

"Can I get you something else to drink?"

"No more wine?"

"I thought you'd had enough."

"I have." She didn't even want any more. She just wanted something to do while she sat there and talked. Something to calm the tension she was feeling, that was building like a storm. She still felt vulnerable sitting there with him, all dressed up in a sequined gown and memories. "How did you know where I went to school?"

"My mother. She kept me well informed. Except for your engagement, that is. She blew that one. How about some coffee? I'd be glad to make a pot."

"No, I'm fine. The caffeine would probably keep me awake."

"It might do you some good."

"I'm afraid I'm not a drinker," she said as, still at loose ends, she ran a finger over a huge quartz rock that was sitting on the coffee table. She'd noticed another larger quartz decorating an end table. Apparently he liked rocks. He'd had them as a kid, too, only smaller, cheaper. "But then you probably already realized that. This is very nice."

"I did notice. And thank you. Are you into rocks?" he asked, nodding at the crystal.

"Into?"

"Some people say they have magical powers, like healing, foretelling the future."

She'd been rubbing a rough spot on the crystal, and now she took her hand away. He had magical powers. If only she could be transported away from there. "Do you believe that?"

"Not really. I just like the way they look. Although that particular one is kind of significant. It's a quartz crystal."

"It's very nice."

"Like the wine?"

"Pardon me?"

"Dyana, this may be way off-base, but would you be uncomfortable with me because you're still angry with me?"

The man was a master of odd questions. "Why would I be angry at you?"

"I don't know . . . the past?"

"That was a long time ago, Chad."

"Yes." He paused. Then he went on in a low, serious tone. "I don't know if you realized it or not, but I've always wanted to tell you that the only reason I stayed with Jeannie Williamson when we broke up was because we had made love."

Dyana's stomach twisted in a tight knot as he spoke. Of all the things he could have mentioned, that was the last thing she expected. She hadn't realized, but that wasn't the point. Although it had happened a long time ago, she carried a lot of excess baggage about that night. It was the only thing she'd ever done as a teenager that she hadn't admitted to her parents. *Oh, by the way, Mom, I made love with Tubbs tonight.*

"I'm sorry, Dyana. I didn't mean to upset you. I just wanted you to know. After that night I knew I wouldn't be able to be with you and stay away from you. I didn't want to ruin your life."

By now her hands were trembling and her stomach churning. She stood again, walking to the windows. She could see her reflection, Chad sitting on the sofa behind her. Although she tried to speak normally, her words came out in a whisper. "You promised never to mention that night, Chad."

"I haven't," he said. "Until now."

It was after they'd made love that they'd argued over the quartz crystal and she'd crushed his spider. Actually they'd argued because they had made love. It had scared them both. They hadn't meant for anything to happen. His parents had been out of town and things had gotten out of hand. Kissing, petting. One thing had led to another. Looking back, it was all so ironic. They'd been old enough to make love and possibly produce a child, and yet they had been children themselves, reading comic books one moment, taking off their clothes the next.

"My sister would have killed me if she'd found out what happened between us," she murmured.

"Your parents wouldn't have been too happy, either," he said.

"They would have been devastated." She'd been sixteen, with her life ahead of her. "But Darcy was always harping at me. She thought we were too young."

"We *were* too young," Chad agreed. Then he added softly, "But we're not too young anymore."

What was that supposed to mean? Dyana could feel him come up behind her. She turned to face him, surprised at how close he was standing, at the serious look on his face. When had things gotten so intimate between them. *How* had things gotten so intimate between them? She licked her lips nervously. "I don't want to be hurt, Chad."

"I won't hurt you."

"That's what you say."

"That's what I mean."

"Chad, you have women all over the world. They're like cars, awarded to you for being MVP of some game. They follow you like you're a gladiator from old Rome and they're the spoils of war."

"Dyana, I won't deny that I have a lot of women in my life. I do. But would it surprise you if I told you they were mostly show?"

That had to be a joke. "Are you saying you're celibate?"

"No." He shook his head. "But I'm not sexually promiscuous, either. To coin a cliché, I don't believe I've ever had a really meaningful relationship, except for a girl in L.A. a couple years back, and she didn't last very long. And you."

That was as hard to swallow as his humility. She gave a short, brusque laugh. "We sound like an ad for safe sex. 'Have you been tested lately? Who are your partners?'"

"What's wrong with that?"

She moved away. "I'm not into sex for the sake of sex."

Chad followed. "Neither am I," he said. "And despite what you obviously think, I'm not into coercing women to my bed."

"Then what are you into?"

"At the moment, you."

"I'm not sure I understand what you mean."

"I'd like to see more of you, Dyana. Why is that so hard to understand?"

It was time to level with him. No, it was time to level with Dyana. She looked at him as she spoke, wanting him to know she meant every word. "You know, Chad, you come here after ten years, discover I'm not married, and come on to me like gangbusters. I'm not sure why. I'm not even sure I believe the story about your mother not telling you about my engagement being broken. You're here in town a lot. Surely you saw other people over the years who told you where I was and what I was doing."

He shook his head. "I heard you were teaching at Meadows. That's it. Not even counseling, Dyana, *teaching*. I'm really not here very often. I come maybe twice a year for a couple of days. And truthfully, I didn't ask anyone about you."

And truthfully, there was the rub. "Why not?"

"You really want to know? Because I didn't want to remember. It seemed something that happened a long time ago, when we were kids, and it was best forgotten."

"But then?" She waited for his answer.

"But then I saw you and changed my mind. Is that a crime?"

She turned from the windows with a sigh. The crime was in not being honest. "No."

"Look, Dyana," Chad said in a lighthearted tone, sighing, too, "we've gotten off to a bad start. This is too serious a subject. How about if we start over? Let's pretend we don't know each other. You've come here, you like the view. We've talked a bit, had some wine." He glanced around the apartment and headed for the stereo. "I'll put on some music."

The man was too suave for his own good. Although she smiled, she had to correct him. "Complication," she said. "I wouldn't have come here if I didn't already know you."

He had bent over the stereo. He paused, half turning to meet her gaze. "You wouldn't?"

"No."

"No music, then?"

She shook her head. "Not if we don't know each other. You could listen by yourself."

"Maybe we met last week?"

She shook her head again. "Not a chance."

"I see." He frowned a moment, studying her, contemplating. "We're stuck with the past, huh?"

"Unfortunately."

"Oh, well." He shrugged. "It was a good try. I may as well put the music on, anyhow." Soft strains of a hit song filled the room. "Dance?"

"We did that at the reunion."

That made him laugh. "Dyana, we did a lot of things at the reunion."

Including kissing. She felt herself start to flush at the memory, but she turned away to pick up her purse and gather her trophy. "I really should go, Chad. I have to get up early."

"What time's the soccer game?"

"Noon."

"That's early?"

"When you're out late it is." She had turned back to him, ready to leave. "It was good seeing you," she said. "Thanks for the wine."

"My pleasure. Sure you want to leave? Considering our past, I mean."

"What?" She wasn't sure she'd heard him right, and she hadn't realized that he had come up behind her again, like at the window.

"Just what I said."

She stood there a long moment. "I—Chad, I have to go."

"I was honest with you before, Dyana. Be honest with me now." This time his voice was husky as he stood mere inches from her. It drove her crazy, his being so close and not touching her. His breath was warm on her neck, sensuous, feathering across to her ear. "Do you really want to leave?"

Poor Cleopatra. She hadn't had a chance, either. And Lois Lane and Juliet had been doomed from the start. Dyana could almost hear the train. She wished he'd close the distance between them, take her in his arms, cart her off to the bedroom, and make mad, passionate love to her. "I can't stay," she murmured. "I really can't, Chad."

"Do you want to go?"

The crime was in not being honest. "No," she admitted at last. "No, I don't want to go."

"Good. I don't want you to go, either."

Wishes, sometimes they came true—for then he did close the distance between them.

CHAPTER
Three

SOMEHOW DYANA KNEW that Chad was going to kiss her. She also knew that this embrace would be different from the others, the explosion greater, the blaze hotter. This was the wildfire waiting for the spark, and as she watched him draw near, her breath hitched in her throat and her stomach fluttered with anticipation.

"Chad, you know this is wrong," she murmured.

He shook his head no. "The only thing wrong about it is that we've spent half the night talking. Believe me, Dyana, it's right. It's very right."

"But it's been so long since we've seen each other."

"All of ten years. Or all of a second, whichever way you want to look at it."

How could he seduce her with his voice? Mesmerize her with his eyes? But he was right. *This* was right; she knew it as well as he did, and she waited for him to take her into his arms. How he could narrow an already narrow gap so slowly was beyond her, but the moment stretched out agonizingly as second by second passed, his arms enfolding her, gathering her tight, his touch feathering along her back, his lips descending—descending on hers.

When their mouths met at last, his lips brushing hers ever so gently, she sighed and leaned into him, overwhelmed by an emotion she couldn't quite identify. Excitement, certainly—and desire. Sweet, wild passion. She'd wanted him to kiss her. She'd wanted more than a kiss. But need and exhilaration weren't what made her feel all shaky inside and frightened, as if something momentous were happening. She couldn't explain it exactly, but his lips felt so good. So satisfying. As if all these years that they had been separated they had been waiting for this moment, and now it was happening. As if it were a matter of destiny.

As if she'd come home.

Chad moaned deep in his throat, too, and clutched her to his length, kissing her with an abandon that was almost frightening in its intensity. His lips were hot and hard and demanding all at the same time, and his hands burned through the fabric of her dress. Even though he was a big man, their bodies fit together perfectly. They'd always fit, and she pressed against him, not teasing, wanting. *Needing*. Desire surged through her like hot oil on a flame. She wanted nothing more than for him to throw her down on the floor and take her right there.

Chad must have felt the same exhilaration. "Dyana," he murmured hoarsely. "God, Dyana, I want you so bad."

They both knew there was no turning back, and neither of them could wait. His hands were everywhere at once: in her hair, holding her head still so that he could plunder her lips; on her back, touching, caressing the bare skin, trailing around to cup her breasts. Dyana matched him move for move. Not pausing to consider what she was doing, she let her hands wander along his

back, down his arms, across his chest. It was too late to
resist now. Or to object. She wasn't even shy about
unbuttoning his shirt and slipping her hands inside. His
chest hairs prickled her palms sensuously. When he
kissed her again, she lolled her head back so that he
could trail a tempestuous path along her jaw, down her
throat, around the neckline of her dress.

"Chad," she murmured, feeling weak and light-
headed. "Oh, Chad."

He responded by kissing her again and again, thrust-
ing his tongue deep in her mouth. Each time their lips
met, she felt more and more impatient and she drew him
closer. With another husky groan he tugged at her dress.
"How the hell do I get this off?" he muttered hoarsely.
"Where's the zipper?"

"On the side."

Although he found the zipper, the dress didn't slip
right off. He had to lift it up, over her head. Because of
all the sequins, it was heavy, in the way, and Dyana
tugged at it, too, wanting it off, wanting to feel him
touching her bare skin, caressing.

"Wait, I've got it." Finally, in one quick movement,
he slipped the gown from her body and tossed it aside.
It landed in a heap at her feet.

Because her dress was black, Dyana was wearing a
matching bra and garter belt and she stood there in the
middle of his apartment, shivering as the night air
curled around her nakedness. She had no idea how she
looked in high heels and skimpy lace, the long expanse
of her legs, the thrust of her breasts. Yet she stood
proudly, legs apart, chest forward as Chad's gaze practically devoured her.

"God, you're beautiful," he whispered huskily.

"Thank you."

"You're welcome." As out of place as their conversation seemed, at the same time it was normal. He held her spellbound with his gaze.

Not quite knowing what else to say, she murmured, "Shall I take off my bra?"

He shook his head. "No, I'll do it."

Dyana thought he would go fast, but he drew this moment out, too, walking toward her again and very slowly removing the wispy garment. He unhitched the delicate snap by degrees, never taking his eyes from her. When her breasts were free, they sprang forward, proud and full. She thrust her shoulders back and waited for him to touch her. But Chad was in absolutely no hurry now. Reaching his hands out, he trailed one finger around the swollen mounds, teasing her, circling her nipples as if he had all the time in the world. She sighed with pleasure when at last he cupped her breasts in his hands.

"Oh, Chad," she moaned, lolling her head back in enjoyment. She clutched at his shoulders as wave after wave of pleasure spread through her. She had forgotten about her garter belt and stockings, until he began to unhook the nylon material and peel it down her legs one at a time. Feeling like a robot, a slave to love, she stepped from her shoes on command. When he stepped back to stare at her, she shivered again, fully naked now.

"Are you cold?" he asked softly. "I tend to keep the air-conditioning at ice-cube level."

She shook her head. "No. Just scared." Why not be honest? There were very few barriers between them now.

"Of me?"

"Of this." The moment.

"I'm sorry. I can take you home if you want."

She gave a half-laugh of disbelief. This was a fine time to offer. "Thanks, but I don't want to go home."

"You're sure?"

"Yes."

"Look at me and say that."

Tossing her head back, she looked directly at him. "I don't want to go home."

"Good." He smiled, that damn cute grin of his, and then he started toward her. "All right, Dyana, if we're going to do this, let's do it right."

Before she could object, he scooped her into his arms as he had earlier and carried her into the bedroom, placing her in the middle of his bed. While she couldn't help but notice that this room was as attractive as the rest of the apartment, she had little time for looking at it. The only thing she was interested in was Chad and the fact that they were going to make love. She'd been honest with him, and with herself. She didn't want to go home. She didn't have any second thoughts about it, no regrets. It was as if once she had decided to stay, the rest was inevitable. And besides, this was her Tubbs, her love.

Chad peeled his clothes from his body, practically ripping them off in his haste. When he was done, he paused beside the bed. Looking at him, she felt as if time had been stripped away and he was standing in front of her in his bedroom that day so many years ago, but then she realized that this was here and now, and they were adults. He was as magnificent naked as he was dressed, perhaps more so. All muscle and power, to Dyana he resembled a prized sculpture, a cross between a dream and Adonis, and he was fully aroused and needing her.

"Ready?" he whispered, sitting beside her on the bed.

"Yes," she answered.

Laying her back gently, it was as if he were intent on memorizing every single inch of her body. Starting all over again, he drew her into his arms and kissed her passionately, moving from her head to her toes in one slow, agonizing caress. No part of her body was left unexplored. When he got to her breasts, she moaned and clutched at him as he went from one nipple to the other, touching, stroking, licking.

"Beautiful," he murmured again, "so very beautiful."

Not even registering his words, Dyana pressed toward him. She was tired of talk. She'd never been a very patient person, and right at the moment she wanted to feel, not converse. Boldly she placed his hand back on her breast. "Don't stop now."

His laugh was husky, pleased. "You like that, do you?"

She swallowed her pride. "Yes."

"And this?" He bent his head to suckle her breasts some more, cupping them in his hands and caressing their fullness.

"Yes," she choked out.

"How about this?" he asked as he slid one hand down her belly to the dark triangle of hair.

Although she'd known what was coming, the pleasure was so intense that she could hardly speak. But he wasn't going to let her off the hook easily. "Dyana?" he murmured. "Do you like that?"

"Yes." God, yes.

Then, shocking her, he kissed her there, too, replacing his hand with his mouth. She gasped with the pleasure as stars exploded in the sky and the universe began to spin away in a wild vortex.

"Chad! Oh, God!" She felt as if she were going to shatter into a thousand pieces, only it was a pleasant sensation, one she could experience over and over again. And she did, tossing her head back and forth as tension racked her body. "Now, Chad," she murmured. "Please, now."

Just before she reached the peak, he nudged her legs

aside and entered her. As if in agony, he paused momentarily, taking a deep breath and lowering his head to her chest.

"Are you all right?" she asked.

"Yes. Just overwhelmed. Give me a minute."

She knew the feeling and she stroked her hands through his hair gently as she waited, burying her fingers in the thick, dark mass. "It's all right, Chad."

He laughed. "You bet it is." Rising slightly, he arched above her. "Hang on tight. Here we go."

He wasn't joking. Dyana gasped as he began the age-old movement, stroking in and out, faster, harder. Tension gripped her again, threatening to spin her away through the galaxy. She was on a roller coaster ride, wild and out of control. Or a train. A runaway train. A steam engine ready to explode.

"Please," she murmured, thrashing her head back and forth. She arched toward him, seeking. Wanting. Needing. "Please, Chad."

"Wait, Dyana." Still he kissed and stroked her, denying her the ultimate.

"Please."

And still.

"Now, Chad!" she demanded, clutching at his shoulder. Without realizing it, she raked her nails down his back. "Please, now."

At last he stroked faster, so fast that she hurtled into space, exploding into a kaleidoscope of colors and sparks. A supernova of enjoyment. Pleasure spread through her in wild, undulating waves.

Chad's body jerked, too, and he collapsed on her. "Oh, God, Dyana," he cried out. "Oh, Lord, you're magnificent."

For the longest time neither of them could move. They lay in bed, their bodies joined, legs intertwined. Dyana could hear his heartbeat, the slow, steady rhythm, his raspy breath returning to normal. Finally he shifted his weight so he wasn't lying on her. "I'm sorry. I'm a little heavy for you."

"You're fine." Yet she let him adjust their bodies so that she was resting her head on his shoulder. He stroked his hand down her bare torso to her hip.

"You were fantastic, Dyana."

He wasn't so bad himself. "Thank you. Did I—did I satisfy you?" It was odd, considering what had just happened between them, considering that she was lying there naked, but she felt funny asking such an intimate question.

"Very much so. Did I satisfy you?"

"Oh, yes."

She flushed when he laughed at the inflection in her voice. "That good? I'm glad." He trailed his hand up her body to her breasts, lingering. "It can be even better, though."

Already a tingle shivered up her spine. "What do you mean?"

"The second time is usually just as good as the first," he said, gently turning her over and nudging her legs apart, "if not better."

Ten years ago there had been no second time, just fear. And arguments. It was better. Actually, it was fabulous. They made love slowly, leisurely. This time Dyana wanted to pleasure him, to give him back a small measure of what he had given her. For all her inexperience, she knew exactly what to do. Taking him in both hands, she began a rhythmic touch that left him gasping in pleasure. "Oh, God, Dyana," he murmured, "I can't wait much longer."

Then he began to kiss her again. All over. Torturing her with his lips, his touch. The universe exploded for her one more time. When they come back to earth, she sighed aloud and snuggled her head on his chest.

"Tired?" Chad asked.

"Very."

"Here I thought maybe we'd work out a bit."

She'd had a moment to look at his bedroom, and she was amazed at the weight-lifting apparatus in the corner. He had nearly a full gym in the bedroom. "I was going to ask you about that," she said. "Why do you have weights here?"

"I have to keep in shape."

"But I thought you weren't here very often."

"When I am here, I have to work out. Football players use weights every day."

"There are more than weights on those machines," Dyana remarked. "That one resembles a torture chamber."

He laughed. "Only the strong survive."

"That sounds gruesome."

"Sometimes it is," he said. "Football's a tough business, Dyana. It's rough and it's violent, but it's fun, too. It does take constant training, lifting, working out, pumping up, eating right. Speaking of eating, how about some scrambled eggs? I'm getting kind of hungry."

"You ate dinner."

"You call that little piece of chicken dinner?"

They'd had chicken Kiev, rice, vegetables, and salad, typical banquet fare. "It wasn't bad."

"It wasn't good, either. And it sure as hell wasn't enough." She flushed when he added, "And besides, I've been working very, very hard." But when he kissed her, she smiled. Springing from the bed, he slipped on his pants. "Here." He tossed her his shirt. "It'll be a little big, but it'll keep you from getting cold. Come on. You can watch me cook."

The shirt was big, striking her at her knees, but

Dyana buttoned it and followed him. It smelled of him, that special scent that was all Chad.

Although it was small, the kitchen was as tasteful as the rest of his apartment. She sat on a stool at the break-fast bar, watching him pad around barefoot and bare-chested, making what he called an orange froth, which consisted of at least a dozen egg whites—the yolks weren't part of his diet—and orange juice, at two in the morning.

"That's not like any diet I've ever been on," she said when he listed some of the food he consumed daily. He'd been in training in high school, but nothing like this. According to Chad, in addition to lifting weights and running, he ate at least a half pound of pasta, a couple servings of rice, potatoes, and bread—no sour cream or butter, though—several pounds of fish or meat, and lots of green, leafy vegetables every single day. Even though it sounded high protein and low fat, it had to be two thousand calories minimum.

"But you're trying to lose weight," he pointed out. "Which, by the way, you don't need to do. You happen to be perfect just the way you are."

"Thank you." She smiled at his compliment.

"I'm trying to stay in shape," he went on. "Can I fix you an egg? I don't eat them per se, but I do know how to cook one."

Dyana shook her head. "I'm really not hungry. I will have some of that coffee, though, if you don't mind fixing it."

"How about some herb tea instead? I wouldn't want you to lie awake all night."

The way he smiled at her, she knew he didn't mean a word. "I'll bet."

He laughed, as she'd known he would. "I said 'lay awake.' It's an interesting prospect, no?"

"Interesting, yes," she answered. "But I do have to

be at the soccer game. Darcy's kids would be disappointed if I didn't show up." Actually Dyana was surprised that it was so early. She thought for sure it was close to dawn.

"Don't worry. I'll let you sleep. I'll even set the alarm, just in case. By the way, where do you live?"

"The suburbs."

"Dyana, in Chicago that encompasses a lot of territory."

"True." She smiled at him in agreement. "But I didn't go far from home. Since I teach at Meadows, I live just a few miles away."

"That makes sense."

"Where do you live in L.A.?"

"In a suburb close to the stadium." When she glanced at him pointedly, he added, "Okay, I agree, that encompasses a lot of territory. Why?"

"I just wondered. The way they give you cars, I thought maybe you had five or six homes."

"I only have two apartments, one here and one there."

"And?" She couldn't help but ask.

"And two cars."

"In addition to the Mercedes and the Lamborghini, or counting them?"

"In addition."

She shook her head in mock disgust. "Chad Weber, what are you going to do if you ever stop playing football?"

"Who says I'm going to stop?"

"Eventually you'll have to retire."

"Eventually," he agreed. "In the meantime I'm just enjoying the perks."

"Including the women?"

He paused, glancing at her. "We already talked about that, didn't we?"

"Yes."

"You don't believe me?"

She just shrugged. She wasn't sure whether she believed him or not. "It really doesn't matter."

"But it does matter," he said seriously. "It matters to me."

She stared at him a long moment. "Chad, did you make love with Jeannie Williamson?"

At first he didn't seem to know what she was talking about. "When we were kids?" Then he shook his head. "No."

"You could have."

"I know, but I didn't."

For some silly reason it pleased her that she'd been the only one, even though it had been ten years ago. It made that night they'd spent together as kids meaningful, and not so awful. "I'm glad."

"So am I." At first he seemed serious, then he grinned, mocking her. "But I have a feeling I would have been in deep trouble if I had."

"That's the only reason?"

"Could there be any other?"

"You're incorrigible, Chad Weber," she said, but she was teasing. Then, still watching him, she said seriously, and very softly, "Just do me one favor, okay?"

"What's that?"

"Let me down easy."

Chad frowned at her as though puzzled by her request. Placing his drink aside, he came to her, tilting her chin up so that she was looking at him. "Dyana, I don't intend to let you down at all."

Promises. She hoped they were like wishes.

The alarm woke her. It was one of those loud, irritating things that didn't stop until it was shut off. She'd always hated electronic clocks. They were so shrill, and she was always subdued in the morning, wanting to snuggle down and snooze for ten minutes more. She'd been dreaming about Chad. They were kids, teenagers again, out in his beat-up car listening to music by moonlight. Everyone had been there, cheering them on. She'd been wearing her sequined dress and they'd danced to their favorite song, which became an ugly noise, a loud, irritating noise, and the night changed to dawn, cold, gray dawn.

Dyana tugged the sheet over her head, but the noise didn't go away. Finally she rose in a fog and turned off the alarm, flopping back on her pillow tiredly. It was so gray outside. She'd had very little sleep last night and the last place she felt like going was a soccer game. But Darcy would be expecting her. And besides, she was alone. It took her several long minutes to acknowledge that no one was in the apartment with her. Neither the television nor the radio was playing, and the stereo was off. The shower wasn't running, there were no noises or tantalizing aromas coming from the kitchen. Just an echo of emptiness. Quiet. Solitude. Where was Chad?

Somehow she knew he was gone—just as she'd known that he was going to kiss her last night—not jogging, not shopping, driving, or working out. *Gone*.

For a moment Dyana didn't know what to think or how to feel. Should she be angry? Hurt? Upset? He had made love to her again last night, declaring words of love. They'd fallen asleep very late. A note was propped beside her pillow, held there with the quartz rock, her name scrawled across the front in bold letters. Was he trying to blow her off? Let her down gently? She tried to think of another reason he would leave, running out and leaving just a note, but she couldn't come up with anything that made sense.

Still lying in his bed, she contemplated the missive. It was on white stationery, written with a green pen. Green. How odd. Yellow was the color of cowards. She couldn't help but wonder what it said. "Gee, thanks, I had a great time." Or "Wow, thanks for the super evening. What a great class reunion."

Sighing, she sat up and pulled the paper from under the rock. May as well get it over with. *Dear Dyana.* The room was cold, making her shiver, but she ignored the temperature and unfolded the note. Several ten-dollar bills fluttered out, onto the bed. She glanced at them, insulted. Surely she was worth more than fifty dollars.

She turned to the note. Chad's handwritting was as bold inside as out, the letters large, distinctive. Green. No *Dear Dyana.* "Didn't want to wake you," it read. "You were sleeping so peacefully. I set the alarm like I promised. Hope you make your soccer game on time— football's better, more of a challenge. Forgot to mention I had to be in L.A. this morning for mini-training camp. Took the early flight out. Here's money for cab fare. Your purse looked too small to contain anything except lipstick. Talk to you soon. Love, Chad. P.S. The night was fabulous."

She'd only missed it by a word or two. Fabulous was just as good as great. *Love, Chad?* That was as odd as the rest of the missive. How could a person "forget" to mention something as important as training camp? It was like forgetting to mention you had a spare arm or a wife and kids.

Maybe he even had those.

But he had just been voted Bachelor of the Year. Or Bachelor of the Decade or Universe or something.

Refusing to acknowledge the hurt, Dyana tossed the sheet aside and got out of bed. His shirt was on the end of the bed, where she'd placed it last night, and his pants were crumpled in a corner, where he'd left them. Someone—Chad, obviously—had hung her sequined dress over one of the dining room chairs. It was all she had to put on. That was one of the disadvantages of staying all night with someone. You had to wear the same clothes home in the morning.

Well, she had to face up to it. She'd stayed, all right. And now he was gone. She could hardly blame him. She'd asked for it. She'd come home with him. She knew the score. She'd known the moment they walked into the place last night what was going to happen between them, and she'd let it barrel along. Making the best of a bad situation, she slipped on her clothes and went into the bathroom to make sense out of her hair. She looked exactly as she'd thought she'd look—a fool —but she had to go out on the street in order to get home. She could at least fix up her face.

After splashing water on her eyes, Dyana moistened her fingers and swept them through her short-cropped hair. She'd never been one to fuss much, so her hairdo was easy to fix. Next she opened the medicine cabinet and found some toothpaste, spreading it on her finger and scrubbing as best as she could. Amazing what a person could do with a little ingenuity. At least it would make her mouth taste good, mint flavored. If only she could mint-flavor the morning, or rather, last night.

The lake was as beautiful in the daytime as at night. As she went through the living room toward the front door, ready to leave, she glanced out the windows at the fluffy clouds and azure water. Odd, betrayal looked the same, too, now or then. She'd been sixteen years old the last time Chad had hurt her, and although she was all grown-up now, this time it hurt just as bad.

Pausing, she swept up her trophy. The one they'd given him sat on the end table beside the other quartz rock. Damn the man. Too bad she didn't have a spider to crush. In all honesty, she had to admit, this time it hurt more.

This time it hurt like hell.

CHAPTER
Four

DYANA HAD ALWAYS assumed that rich people slept late in the mornings, especially on Sunday mornings. Given the number of people milling about in the lobby of Chad's building, all dressed in designer tennis attire or jogging suits, apparently that philosophy was flawed. Where in the world were they going? Surely not to exercise. Not a single person looked like they were ready to work up a sweat.

They must have wondered the same thing about her. Several tenants glanced her way, flashing tight little smiles of curiosity. Knowing she looked ridiculous dressed in her sequined gown at this time of day and not caring—well, she really *did* care, she was just feeling angry and perverse, considering the way she'd been dumped. Duped, rather?—she flashed a smile back, swinging through the lobby with her trophy as if she were footloose and fancy-free. She'd dried her eyes and put on a happy face, and it wasn't as if she had anything else to lose. After all, what was a girl's reputation?

When she got to an attractive, dark-haired man sitting at a desk near the door—a security guard, no doubt—she smiled at him, too, and said, "It's a tough job, but somebody's gotta do it. You know, mornings are real bummers in these buildings. If a guy would just give a girl a chance."

She had assumed he would have a fit, or at least react to her innuendo, but she may as well have been talking to one of the little green monitors he watched. The man smiled back politely, indulgently, obviously ignoring her implication. "The doorman will help you get a taxi, Miss Kincaid. He's right outside."

She paused. "How did you know my name?"

"Mr. Weber described you before he left for the airport this morning. He wanted to make sure we helped you get a taxi home. You're ready to leave?"

What did he think she was doing, looking for tricks? But she was more irritated with Chad than with this man. How presumptuous of him. Who the hell did he think he was, her keeper? "My, my, isn't that nice of Mr. Weber? Thank you, but I can get my own taxi."

"Yes, ma'am, we know you can," the man answered, "but we'll take care of it."

"Excuse me?" The no-nonsense way he made the claim took her aback. No arguments and very polite but very firm. The Miss Manners School of Etiquette, the Nelson Rockefeller School of Charm. And the FBI School of Toughness.

Opening the door for her, he signaled the doorman and went on as if she hadn't even spoken, "We'll take care of it, ma'am, and you won't need to worry about a gratituity."

"Mr. Weber gave you a tip?" She knew he had, she just wanted confirmation.

"Yes, ma'am, he gave us fifty dollars."

That meant her price had been uppcd to a hundred, better than fifty, but still, Marc Antony had given Cleopatra the entire Roman army. But there was no sense in arguing. She went out the door and climbed into the cab.

She lived in the northwest suburbs of Chicago, otherwise known as the land beyond O'Hare. The area had developed into one of the most properous of the city, as well as one of the most lovely. Wide expanses of lawn and attractive buildings compensated for the inconvenience of driving into the city. She didn't have to drive far to her job, though. The high school was just around the corner from her apartment complex. Since she was single, she hadn't put too much into the place, preferring to invest her money in high-yield funds and wait for the time when she could buy a house. If all went well, next year she could afford something small.

In the meantime her apartment had to do. It was tiny —three rooms, a kitchen, a living room, and a bedroom—but it was cozy and reflected her personality. Cluttered, Darcy liked to say, like Dyana's mind. Which at the moment was seething with anger. The more she thought about last night and Chad, the angrier she became. How could he walk out like that? Just up and leave?

Damn the man. Again.

Silently cursing him as well as whoever was calling her and making her rush, she pushed the key in the door and hurried to answer the phone. She didn't even get to say hello. The moment she picked it up, Susan started talking: "Dyana! You're home. It's about time. I've been calling all night long. Wait. I'll be right there. I'm coming over for a blow-by-blow."

"I'm going to a soccer game," Dyana said.

There was a long pause. "A soccer game? This is important."

"So's the soccer game."

"Dyana, no soccer game in the whole wide world is

as important as your best friend knowing what happened between you and the sexiest man alive."

"What's to know?"

Susan almost choked. "What's to know? What happened, that's what! Where've you been all night? What did you do? He carted you off in his Mercedes."

"He took me to his apartment."

"And?"

"And we spent the night together," Dyana said simply. No sense hiding it. She'd already admitted she was a fool.

Susan paused again, in surprise this time, or else in deep thought. She gave a heavy sigh. "And you're home? It must not have gone too well."

Dyana should have realized she couldn't fool her friend. "Why do you say that?"

"Because you're home. Okay, what happened?"

The actual events weren't really important, except to her, and although she'd acted casual about the whole business, in actuality it was the last thing Dyana wanted to talk about, even to Susan. "I just told you what happened. We spent the night together."

"That's the problem. You're so blithe about it all. Did you go to bed with him or not?"

One of Susan's bad points was her blunt attitude. Everything was cut-and-dried. Yes or no. "That's a little personal, don't you think?"

"So you did go to bed with him," she said, answering her own question. "Wasn't he any good?"

Blunt was one thing, her question quite another. "Susan, I am not going to answer those kinds of questions. In fact, I'm not going to answer any questions. I'm late for the soccer game. Good-bye."

"Wait! Dyana, don't hang up," Susan said in a rush. "What?"

She didn't want to talk anymore, but apparently her

friend did. "Look, you're upset, and I don't want you to be alone. I'll meet you at Darcy's house. That's where you're going after the soccer game, isn't it?"

"I'm not upset."

"Dammit, Dyana, something's wrong. I can tell. I know you, and you're too cool."

All morning long Dyana had pretended that if she didn't acknowledge the pain, it wouldn't exist. It wasn't a bad ploy, except it didn't always work when sympathetic friends called. Talking to Susan, she felt like someone had smashed a fist into her stomach. The hurt went deep, aching terribly. "It was no big deal."

"I don't believe you."

"I'm fine," she insisted.

"Sure, and I'm the Queen of Sheba. I'll meet you at the soccer field instead. We'll talk there."

"Susan, I do not want to talk about Chad," Dyana warned.

"Okay."

Susan was so agreeable, Dyana knew she was lying. "I don't."

"I know. We'll just talk."

"And I'll cry."

"It might do you some good. He must have been a real jerk."

"I was the idiot," Dyana said.

"I'll be right there."

"See you in a bit." Dyana sighed, knowing it wouldn't matter even if she objected. Susan would come, anyhow. In the meantime she had to face Darcy, too. Her sister had been as excited about the class reunion as she'd been, for very similar reasons, namely that she'd wanted Dyana to see Chad again. And her sister could read her way too easily.

Although she was running late, Dyana took a shower and changed into jeans and an old, beat-up sweatshirt before she left. It struck her just below the hips and felt wonderfully saggy and out of shape. She didn't wear much makeup ordinarily, and she scrubbed her face clean and squiggled her fingers through her damp hair, letting it curl around her face. She'd always been a wash-and-go type person, casual, and there was no reason at the moment to make an exception. Last night she'd been all dressed up, and look what had happened.

Opening her closet, she tossed the sequined dress on the floor. It was an unpleasant reminder of her stupidity, and she didn't want to see it again. She went into the kitchen to fix a quick sandwich before she left, and out of habit she flicked on the television. Chad was the last person she expected to see, but there he was, on the news, disembarking the airplane in Los Angeles. She glanced at her watch. It was after twelve here, only ten in the morning there. Either he had to have taken a very early flight or some kind of supersonic jet.

As usual he was gorgeous, wearing slacks and a casual shirt, his hair falling appealingly over his forehead, and his smile so engaging. The cheerleaders that met him thought he was gorgeous, too. They ran and hugged him, kissing him, surrounding him with their little pom-poms and skimpy outfits. The Crusading Angels, they were called.

Damn, damn, damn him!

Dyana flicked off the set and instead of fixing a sandwich, she grabbed a chocolate bar from the freezer. She kept them to reward herself in times of stress, and considering that she'd managed not to smash the television into a thousand pieces—a supreme effort—she was certainly deserving.

Darcy was almost as well groomed as Chad. When Dyana got to the soccer field, her sister was wearing slacks and a casual top, but her long blond hair was pulled back from her face and she had applied makeup so artfully, she looked more like a cover girl than a wife and mother. The other women had to hate her. She'd had three children and hadn't gained an ounce of excess weight. She was pacing the sidelines with her husband, Phillip, watching her offspring run up and down, kicking at a ball. Dyana couldn't help it. Every time she saw the two of them together, she smiled. They were always holding hands or touching.

"Don't you guys ever get sick of all that mushy stuff?" she teased, plastering a smile on her face. If she could help it, Darcy would not guess that she was upset! "Sorry I'm late. I got caught in traffic."

"On a Sunday?" Phillip frowned at her. Dyana's brother-in-law was what was commonly known as a hunk—tall, dark, and handsome. Brilliant. He was a nice guy, too, and usually he could read her well. Unfortunately he was slipping today—or he wasn't going to let her get away with her fib.

"Amazing, isn't it?" she answered. "The cars just get worse and worse around here."

"I tried to call you this morning," Darcy said, coming to greet her with a kiss on the cheek and a hug. "You must have left already."

The phone must have gotten a workout. First Susan, then Darcy. "I had some errands to run." Not wanting to go into the subject of where she'd been last night, Dyana shielded her eyes and glanced at the field. She hadn't been joking when she'd talked with Chad; she knew next to nothing about soccer. The kids were all in a big group running. "How's the game going? Who's winning?"

"Nobody yet," Darcy answered. "Still practice." When she turned to glance toward her children, a soft smile stole over her face. "But Mandy's game's first today. She's going to play center forward."

At nine, Mandy was the eldest of the three children,

tall and blond like her mother. One day she would be just as stunning. "Is that good?" Dyana asked.

"Oh, yes, she's thrilled. She's been practicing a lot, and Missy and Phillip are both envious. Can you stay for all the games?"

Melissa was seven, and always trying to compete with her older sister. Phillip, Jr., was the youngest, only five, but a pure delight, that is to Dyana, since he was a devilish little kid, very much like her, always getting into some kind of trouble.

"Sure, I can stay all day. Why? Got something planned?"

"No, but you look tired."

Just when Dyana had let down her guard, Darcy had come up with a zinger. Dyana shrugged. "I'm tired. I was out late."

"So how did it go?" Darcy seemed excited. She smiled, giving Dyana her total attention. "Last night was your class reunion, wasn't it? You haven't mentioned a thing."

"It was fine."

"Really? Great. I had so much fun at my ten-year reunion. How was Tubbs? Did you see him?"

"Yes, he was there."

"And?"

"He's fine."

"That's it?"

Dyana shrugged. "What else is there? He's playing football."

"I know that." Darcy looked disappointed. "Where's his family?"

"Winnetka."

"That's not far."

"No."

"Did anything happen between you?

"No."

Darcy sighed heavily. "I'm sorry."

Dyana frowned at her. "Why would you be sorry?"

"You know, I always felt guilty for keeping you two apart. I thought that maybe if I hadn't been so strict with you when you were going out with him, things would have worked out differently. Certainly Mom and Dad would have given you a lot more freedom. And he *is* still single," Darcy added.

So that was the impetus. Dyana smiled. "Things worked out just fine," she said. "I'm happy. They gave me the Old Maid award."

"Terrific."

"It was." But apparently she had to convince her sister. "Darcy, I've told you before, I don't mind being single," she went on. "Marriage isn't the big deal it was years ago."

"Marriage will always be a big deal," Darcy said.

Dyana gave her a nod of concession. "Yes, but you know what I mean. It's certainly not the end-all and be-all of a woman's existence. I'm glad you've got a husband and kids. Phillip's wonderful, and I know you're happy, but I'm happy, too. I've got school, the kids, a great career. I'm going to buy a house. I've traveled. What more could I want?"

What she'd always wanted: Chad.

Good grief, how ridiculous. They'd spent one night together and she was acting as if they were great lovers.

Darcy smiled and she looked relieved. "Are you happy? Really? Oh, Imp, I hope so." Imp was Darcy's pet name for her. "I don't mean to harp at you. I just want the best for you."

"I know."

"I love you." She squiggled a hand through Dyana's hair like she had when they'd been growing up. Back then it had irritated Dyana. Now she realized it was an endearment.

"I love you, too," she answered. Despite the fact that her sister was being overprotective, Dyana was touched. And she was glad she didn't have to answer the question about really being happy. "Now," she went on, "tell me about playing center forward in a soccer game. Is that special?"

"Yes. But Phillip knows more about it than I do."

"Does he know about soccer in general?"

"I believe so. Why?"

"Because I think I just might learn how to play."

"You?"

"I'm a good sportswoman," Dyana said in her defense. The tone of Darcy's voice had been almost insulting.

Her sister just laughed. "Unless you lose. Then you're a bad sport. Besides, you're too impetuous to play any kind of organized game. You might run off with the ball."

"Maybe it's time I got hard-hearted." Although she wished she hadn't spoken so sharply, Dyana couldn't help the edge that crept into her voice.

Darcy paused. "Are you sure nothing's wrong, Dyana? Did everything go all right last night?"

"Everything went fine. I'm fine." Dyana shoved her hands into her jeans pockets and glanced at the soccer field. "So. Apparently the object is to kick the ball into the net at the end of the field. Tell me, what are the rules?"

Darcy frowned. "Rules?"

"Who's who? And what they're doing."

As it turned out, Darcy knew as much about soccer as Dyana. Phillip was more of a help, inundating her with rules and regulations and going over the finer points. She was almost sorry she'd asked. She soon discovered that soccer was a variation of rugby and that it had been founded in 1863, long before American football had ever gotten off the drawing boards. The object was to kick or "head"—with your head—a spherical ball into the net at the end of the field but without touching it with your hands. The other object was to keep the opposing team from doing the same thing. All in all, it didn't seem terribly complicated, once you knew all the rules. Somebody was always running and kicking, and the game went very fast.

Susan arrived by halftime, wanting to talk, but Dyana wasn't about to be drawn into a discussion of Chad. Not ever again would she speak of the man, not unless she became as famous as the Brazilian soccer star, Pele. Then she would challenge Chad to a soccer game.

Susan laughed when Dyana mentioned it. They'd walked to the end of the field together, watching as Mandy made a goal. Phillip and Darcy were jumping up and down, hugging each other and screaming. "And then what?"

"I'll kick the ball into his gorgeous buns."

"Revenge is so sweet."

"Hmm, yes," Dyana agreed. "Unfortunately it will never happen. But the girl's soccer team at school needs a coach. Maybe I'll volunteer."

"Whatever makes you happy."

There it was again, that word *happy.* "Yes, whatever."

"Well, obviously you don't want to talk about Chad," Susan went on. "So. Do you want me to stick around?"

"Only if you want to watch Phillip Junior get into trouble. His game is next. Last week he was red-carded. I didn't know what that meant then."

Susan grimaced. "Whatever it is, it doesn't sound great. Besides, the kid isn't old enough for me to ogle, and the refs are all wearing wedding rings. I've got some shopping to do. If you don't need my shoulder, I believe I'll get lost."

"Have fun." Dyana smiled.

"Sure you're okay?"

She smiled again. "Absolutely."

"Liar."

"Want me to flood the field with tears? So he made love to me and walked out. I'll live."

Susan shook her head. "You're too nice, Dyana, you know that? If it were me, I'd fly to L.A. with my soccer ball and for sure kick him in the butt. Catch you later."

That was exactly what she wanted to do, but over the years she had tempered her impulses.

Dyana spent the rest of the afternoon watching soccer and learning about the game. She got home late. Most of the time she'd managed not to think about Chad, at least not every other moment. The phone was ringing again when she walked in. Assuming Susan was being bothersome, she picked it up, only to feel her stomach start to flip-flop at the sound of his low, sexy voice. "You're home," he drawled. "Boy, that was one long soccer game."

"Chad?" Dyana knew darn well it was him. She just had to say his name to get her bearings. She almost hung up, but she was curious. "What do you want?"

If he noticed her cold tone, he ignored it. "I tried to call you when I landed at the airport this morning, but no one answered. In fact, I've been calling most of the day."

She wanted to ask him how he'd dialed the phone with all the women at his side. Instead she said, "How'd you get my number?"

"The operator."

"Why?"

"Why what?" He didn't seem to understand.

"Why did you call?"

"I wanted to make sure you got home all right."

"I did fine."

"Good, I was worried. Did the doorman help you find a cab?"

"Yes. Thank you for the money," she said grudgingly. It had galled her to take it, but he'd been right, last night she hadn't had anything in her purse except a lipstick, her driver's license, and a few dollar bills.

"My pleasure."

A lot of other things had been his pleasure, too. "Excuse me, Chad," she said, "but it's late here. I have to go. Was there anything else you wanted?"

"Not really. I just wanted to talk. Dyana, is something wrong?"

"Whatever makes you think that?"

"You seem upset."

"That's just a tad wrong. I'm furious. Good-bye, Chad. Thanks for the fun time. Last night was fabulous." Without waiting, she clicked the phone down and went into the other room. Seconds later it rang again.

"Dyana?" he said when she picked it up. "I think we were cut off."

She nearly laughed. With an ego like his, it would never occur to him that she'd disconnected them. "We weren't cut off, Chad. I hung up."

She could tell from the pause that he was puzzled. "But why?"

"The same reason you left this morning. I'm busy."

"Look, I'm sorry," he said. "I know I should have mentioned that I had to leave. But there never seemed to be an appropriate moment. What was I going to say, 'I'm glad we're making love, but I have to leave in the morning'?"

"Actually, that sounds pretty good, Chad. It certainly would have been the decent thing to do. You wanted honesty from *me*."

"I didn't mean to be dishonest. It just wasn't a good subject."

"Because you knew I might not have stayed."

The line was silent a long moment. "Maybe," he said. At least he was being honest now, partially, anyway.

"I wouldn't have stayed," she said.

"But you did."

"Yes, I certainly did." And now she had to deal with it. "Look, I've got to go."

"Wait, Dyana, don't hang up yet. I need to talk with you."

"What do you need to know?"

"First, when will I see you again?"

"Never. Second?"

"Dyana, I've apologized once. Don't you understand? I have to be here. I'm a football player. This is my job."

"Oh, I understand. I understand quite well. Now here's something for *you* to understand. I don't want to see you or talk to you or think about you. Good-bye." With that she clicked the phone down again. Only to pick it up when he called back. "Chad, what do I have to do to get it across to you that I don't want to talk to you? I want to go to bed. It's late."

His voice was urgent, impatient. "We have to talk, Dyana. We have to clear this up."

"There's nothing to clear up."

"Yes, there is. You're hurt."

"Don't be silly," she said, her tone facetious. "I'm not hurt. Why should I be hurt? Just because you used me? Tell me, Chad, how often *are* you in Chicago?"

"I live and work here. But I plan to be there a lot now."

"For me?"

"For us."

"Oh, please, Chad, don't. Don't make it worse."

"Dyana, I'd like to get to know you."

How much more did he need to know? "Along with the hundreds of other women in your life?" she asked. "Answer this one, Chad: How many women have you kissed since you got out of bed with me this morning?"

"Did you see the cheerleaders?" He sighed heavily. "You must have seen the cheerleaders. I'm sorry, Dyana. Look, that was a publicity stunt. Pure hype. That's all. It didn't mean a thing."

"What a waste, and you kiss so well." She hung up a third time. When the phone started to ring again, she unfastened the cord from the wall jack. One of the advantages of the newer telephone systems were the mix-and-match parts. A cord in here, a cord out there. He could call all night long for all she cared. It wouldn't bother her. *He* didn't bother her. She wouldn't let him. As far as she was concerned, Chad Weber didn't even exist. She wasn't going to think about him or talk about him anymore. Or talk *to* him. She was going to coach soccer and forget she'd ever seen him or heard from him. And right at the moment she was going to find a spot for her trophy.

CHAPTER
Five

NOT THINKING ABOUT Chad was easier to say than to do. In fact, for the next two weeks Dyana thought of little else. It seemed as if everything in the world happened in Los Angeles, from earthquakes to fires to famous movie stars picketing the Hollywood studios, all reminding her of him.

And, of course, every television sports program, radio station, and newspaper known to man carried an interview with Chad Weber, star lineman for the Crusaders. It got so that she dreaded hearing the news of the day. She almost hoped that if disaster had to happen it would befall New York or Chicago or Atlanta or even Hoboken, New Jersey. Anything to take her mind off the fact that the man was awesome and the night they'd spent together unforgettable.

At first he'd tried calling again. When she'd hooked up the phone the next day, he got through right away, but she hung up. Then he sent her a telegram. She ripped it up without even opening it. He wired flowers, and although they were lovely and she hated doing it, she tossed them in the garbage. She gave the chocolates

—grudgingly—to Susan and the champagne to her neighbor. Once his roommate called, but when the guy mentioned Chad, she pretended to be someone else.

By the time a week went by, she was pretty sure he was going to leave her alone. True to her word, she volunteered to coach the girls' soccer team. It was August, but school was about to start in a few weeks, and the teams were allowed to practice. Because she was a counselor, she had to be in the building, anyhow, so it was no trouble to run scrimmages in the afternoons. Only she still didn't know much about soccer. She supposed she was better than no coach, though, which was what they would have had if she hadn't come forward.

Still, she wished she was better prepared. The day was hot and humid, and she'd been practicing the girls for several hours. In between times, she fought with the football coach over everything imaginable. They had to share a field that day, and for some reason she couldn't figure out why, he wanted to be rid of her and her squad.

But Dyana wasn't about to give in. She didn't have much equipment, but what she had she lined up across the field marking off her practice field. She supposed it was frustration that made her shout at a player. "Dammit, Julie," she yelled when the girl missed a shot. "You're supposed to kick the ball, not look at it. Let's try that over again. And stop worrying about the boys. They're doing just fine on their part of the field."

"You're a real slave driver, Dyana Kincaid."

Chad? Dyana turned to him, shocked. She'd thought about him so much this week, surely she was seeing an apparition. But this was no apparition in front of her, this was flesh-and-blood man, tall and lean and gorgeous, grinning at her like a Cheshire cat.

"Hello," he said. "How are you?"

But Dyana was angry, suddenly furious, and she

glared at him. "What the hell are you doing here?"

He arched an eyebrow. "Still upset with me, I see."

Amazing how he'd guessed. "You didn't answer my question," she said. "What are you doing here, Chad?"

He shrugged, his broad shoulders lifting casually. "I believe it was 'what the *hell* am I doing here?' I had a couple days off. When I last spoke to your sister, she mentioned that the girls' soccer team was in danger of usurping the football squad for the homecoming game. I thought I'd better come by and give the guys some hints."

She gestured toward the other end of the field. "The boys are over there."

"I can see that," he answered, still grinning. "They're pretty hard to miss. You're hard to miss, too. Haven't you noticed everyone looking at you?"

She glanced from the football team to her girls. What did he mean by that? "Why?"

"You look cute when you're sweating, Dyana. But it *is* revealing."

Revealing? For the first time she glanced down at herself. Like her girls, she was wearing shorts and a tank top, which were both soaking wet. Although she had on a bra, her breasts were clearly outlined in the thin material, and her long, limber legs were covered with a sheen of perspiration. She flushed. How embarrassing. Apparently the boys had noticed, too. "You could close your eyes."

"That's like asking me not to breathe."

"Try panting."

"I am."

He knew what she meant. She glared at him and at her girls, who had stopped to stare at him, enthralled. "Miss Kincaid, is that Chad Weber?" one of them whispered.

"Get back to work," Dyana answered. "Julie, you missed the kick again."

"You really are one tough coach," Chad remarked again when the girls had gone on down the field, looking over their shoulders the entire time and whispering among themselves. "I thought you didn't know anything about soccer."

She turned back to him. "A person can learn. And what's wrong with being tough?"

"Nothing, if it's done right. Compliments work, too. She came in good on that shot."

"Yes, she did come in good," Dyana said, "but she still missed. I give compliments—when they're earned." Who did he think he was to come here and question her?

"But the object is to win?"

She wondered what he was getting at. "Isn't that the purpose of the game?"

"Not to me, particularly not at the high school level. Good sportsmanship and learning the game are the things I consider important."

"I'll teach them that."

"I'm just making suggestions, Dyana. You don't have to take it personally."

She put her hands on her hips, tired of his harping. "You know, Chad, there's this old adage: Unless you're willing to do the job, don't criticize."

"Ouch." He held his heart, pretending to be hurt. "Your sister told me you were touchy."

That was another thing she wanted to talk to him about. "Speaking of which," she said, "when did you talk to my sister?" The first time he'd mentioned Darcy, it had gone over her head. Now she wondered just what he was up to.

"The last time I spoke to her was last night," he answered. "But we talk almost daily. Why?"

"That was going to be my question."

He shrugged again. "That's easy. You won't talk to me."

"So you call my sister?" It didn't make sense.

"She's been very helpful."

Dyana shook her head in frustration. "Chad, I don't know what you're trying to pull, but it won't work. What the hell is it that you want from me?"

"You want me to tell the truth?"

"Of course."

"I want you to marry me."

At first she wasn't certain she had heard him correctly. Then she laughed. *"What?"*

"I want you to marry me."

She'd heard it, all right. She shook her head again, in disbelief this time. "Are you feeling well, Chad?"

"I'm fine, why?"

"You just asked me to marry you."

"I know. What's your answer?"

Dyana was still in shock. "You're joking."

"No." ˙

"Chad, we hardly know each other."

"I pointed out two weeks ago that we've known each other all our lives. But I do know what you mean. It's been a while since we've seen each other. I've got a couple days before I have to be in L.A. for the first exhibition game. We could go away if you want. I agree that we need to talk."

Dyana stood on the field, sweaty and dirty, holding her clipboard of names, trying to make sense of the situation. This was not happening. Not to her, Dyana Kincaid, average person, and certainly not in Rolling Meadows, Illinois. "Where?" she asked.

"It's in L.A."

The exhibition game. "No," she said. "I mean, where would we go?"

"The Delmarva Peninsula. You'll love it. It's a stretch of land in the Chesapeake Bay that borders the coast of Delaware, Maryland, and Virginia. Delmarva."

She got it. "I've never heard of it."

"That's because you live in the Midwest. It's a great place for fishing. I understand it's also very romantic, and not terribly touristy. One of the guys on the team owns a condo there. We could go for the weekend."

"The weekend?"

"Actually, a long weekend," he clarified. "Tomorrow's Friday, and I thought we'd leave in the morning."

"I have a soccer team to coach."

"Okay, we'll leave Saturday morning, then," he said. "Or we could go Friday afternoon after practice. We'll still have plenty of time. We can come back Sunday night. I'm sure I can catch a late flight out of O'Hare to L.A."

She frowned, still confused. She couldn't believe she was planning a getaway, standing here and talking about going off with him. It was ridiculous. The whole conversation was ridiculous. Ludicrous. Incongruous. "This is stupid, Chad."

"Why?"

"First of all, I'm not going away with you. Secondly, if I ever did go away with you, it wouldn't be to a condo. I would never stay with you in a condo again."

"Where would you stay?"

She laughed. Didn't he understand? "If I were to stay anywhere, which I'm not," she emphasized again, "it would be a hotel room. A separate room."

He nodded. "Okay. That's fair. A hotel it is."

"You weren't listening, Chad," she said. "I told you I wasn't going."

"I already arranged for the tickets. By the way, I

thought I'd wait for you and we could drive to Darcy's house together. I'm not sure of the way."

She frowned at him again, now following. "Tonight?"

"Yes, tonight."

"Why are you going to Darcy's?"

"For dinner. She's having a barbecue. Did you forget?"

"No, of course I didn't forget," she said. "When did you get invited?"

"Last week. I think she's having my folks, too. She asked for their phone number. And your parents are going to be there. Didn't you know?"

"No." When had all these plans been made? "Well, Darcy can just have them all to herself," she snapped, turning on her heel to stalk off. "I'm not going."

"And miss seeing my folks? They're looking forward to visiting with you."

She spun back around, glaring at him. "Chad, I don't believe you're doing this. Why are you doing this?"

"Doing what?"

"Crowding me. Forcing me. You've come here and taken over my life, expecting me to go away with you —to *marry* you, for God's sake—and you seem to think it's normal."

"Weren't you just angry at me for leaving you the other morning?"

What was he getting at? "Yes."

"Then I don't understand what you're upset about now. I've asked you to marry me."

"It's not normal, Chad."

"Sure it is. True, I am kind of aggressive," he admitted. "I'm a football player and that's my lifestyle. But, believe me, there is nothing wrong with asking someone to marry you when you're in love, Dyana."

If possible, she was even more stunned. "What?" she seemed to be stuck on that word.

"I'm not afraid to admit it," he said. "It's a little scary at first, but I'm in love with you. I finally figured out that I always have been in love with you. I think you love me, too, if you'd just take a moment to calm down and stop being so cranky about everything."

For a moment she was too stunned to speak. This was happening so fast, too fast, and she didn't have time to digest it all. "You love me?"

"Why is that so surprising?"

"You haven't seen me in ten years."

Chad lifted his broad shoulders in another shrug. "You really are bothered by that, aren't you? All right, no problem. I'll admit that was a mistake on my part. We could have been together all this time. Does that make you feel better?"

"No, it doesn't make me feel better," she answered, her voice rising sharply. "I don't want you to *admit* anything, Chad. I don't understand what's going on."

He flashed his famous grin. "That's easy, Dyana. I came here to ask you to go away with me, and to marry me, and you're in the middle of coaching a soccer team, which I must say is a real kick in the teeth—a star football player's wife coaching a soccer team is not going to go over well—and we're going to go to your sister's for dinner as soon as you finish up with practice." He paused, looking down at her. "You will be able to take a shower before we leave?"

"What?" How insulting!

"You *are* dirty." She almost threw her clipboard at him, but he ducked and started backing away. "Meet you by the car. I'm going to go help the football coach."

Good riddance. She was glad to see him go. Except that she had lost her concentration. So had her girls. They were more intent in Chad and on giggling than on practice. They didn't even ask who he was anymore. They *knew*, and all they could do was stare at him as he strolled across the field to the football team.

"Oh," one of them said swooning. "I quit soccer. I'm going out for the football team."

"They don't take girls, egghead," someone else said.

Dyana just pursed her lips and tried to get back into their routine. After five more minutes of frustration she dismissed the team. There was no sense in continuing. Besides, like her girls, she was more concerned about Chad. It occurred to her that in a roundabout way she had agreed to go away with him. It also occurred to her that the reason she had agreed was because she *wanted* to go away with him. What was the matter with her? Wasn't one hurt enough? He was rich and famous and gorgeous, and consequently not the kind of man to settle down with someone like her. Miss Average Hometown Girl.

She sighed. There was no sense in pretending, either. If she were Dorothy, she'd click her heels on purpose. Hell, she'd already been Cleopatra.

Although Dyana had hoped that he would leave and make her life easier, Chad waited for her by the car. Even if she'd wanted to, she couldn't have missed him. He had pulled his red Mercedes alongside her Ford Fiesta and he lounged around carelessly, signing autographs or talking to kids who stopped to ask him questions, his long lanky legs stretched out, hands crossed over his broad chest.

She didn't speak. Since she was still feeling resentful, knowing he wanted to take his car, she climbed in hers and started the engine. "Hey, wait a minute, Dyana," he said, opening the passenger door. "What's the hurry?"

She stared straight ahead, refusing to glance at him. "Dinner."

"You look nice."

"Thank you." She'd showered in the girls' locker room and changed to the sundress she'd worn to school that morning. It was a soft yellow color with little pink flowers, and it fit her bodice tightly, flaring out at the waist.

"You smell nice, too. Perfume?"

"Soap."

"Look," he went on when she didn't bother to say anything more. "Why don't we take my car?"

"I like mine."

"Still mad at me?"

"No."

"Can you wait until I put up the top and lock up?"

"No."

"Someone will steal it."

She looked at him finally and smiled, but it was an expression of sarcasm rather than humor. "That's what happens when you drive a Mercedes. Now, if you were driving a Ford Fiesta like me, you wouldn't have to worry about a little thing like where you go or what you do."

"Why are you still mad at me?"

"I'm not still mad at you."

"Yes, you are. And I haven't done a thing."

What did he call coming here and disrupting her life? What did he call making love to her and walking out?

Hurting her?

He sighed, obviously realizing she wasn't about to give in, and climbed inside her car. The small compact was made smaller by his presence. He took up the entire passenger seat, his shoulders so broad, they almost touched hers. "Let's go, James."

Suddenly she felt guilty, making him leave his car. Whether or not it had been given to him, it had to have cost tens of thousands of dollars and she would have hated to see it stolen. "Will it be all right?"

"My car?" He didn't seem overly distraught. "Look at the bright side," he said. "At least this is the suburbs. Considering the low crime rate, I might have an hour before it's hot-wired."

Purposely sighing louder than he had, she shut off the engine of the Fiesta and climbed out. "Fine. We'll take your car."

Wisely, Chad didn't gloat. He didn't speak much, either, on the way to Darcy's—another wise move on his part. Dyana didn't know why, but she was spoiling for a fight, and she was just waiting for him to make a remark. One remark. She would take great pleasure in blasting him.

But they got all the way to her sister's house without speaking, except for her to give him directions. Darcy lived close by, in one of the nicer subdivisions. The large, rambling homes were all set far back on well-manicured lawns, the architectural style simple yet attractive. As far as Dyana could tell, everyone else was already there. She recognized Darcy's station wagon, and her parents' car sat next to the white Lamborghini Chad had given his folks, which had created quite a stir. Half the neighborhood was out, watching Chad's father open and close the doors.

The Webers hadn't changed much from the last time Dyana had seen them. They were still warm and friendly. Both of them hugged her, talking excitedly about how she had changed, the times she and Chad had gone out together. Funny how that dichotomy worked. Instead of growing dimmer, the memories of the past seemed to increase with age.

Dyana's parents were equally enchanted with Chad, hugging him and complimenting him on his accomplishments, as did every person who had gathered on the driveway, awed to actually meet him in person.

Children milling about asked for his autograph, and Phillip, Jr., brought out a football for Chad to sign. Melissa and Mandy stood staring at him and giggling, making Dyana wonder why little girls were so obnoxious and when they became that way. Even Darcy and Phillip were friendly and welcoming. Didn't they remember the things he had pulled with her as a teenager? Of course, Chad had been her voice of reason back then, tempering her wilder impulses.

Finally they all adjourned to the backyard. Darcy had planned a cookout. Dyana knew it was because she couldn't cook. Neither she nor her sister had ever been great in the kitchen, and even though Darcy was married, her culinary skills hadn't improved at all over the years, so she was always happy when Phillip could help her grill.

Several appetizers sat on the picnic table, a donation from their mother, Dyana was sure, since they tasted delicious. She picked one up, but Darcy slapped her hand and passed the platter to Chad, who had settled in a lawn chair next to his parents.

"How did mini-camp go?" she asked him as he selected a few meatballs. "Are you ready for football season?"

"I think so. We look pretty good this year. I'm counting on have a good shot at the division championship."

"My, Darcy, when did you start following football?" Dyana asked curiously, albeit a bit sweetly.

"I've always followed football." Her sister's smile was genuinely sweet, which made Dyana feel guilty. She had to stop being such a witch. She was angry at Chad, not her family. "I can't say that I understand it," Darcy went on in her cute manner, "but I watch it. And now that I'm married, I watch it even more."

"It never fails," Dyana's father popped in. "Women

always complain about men watching sports."

"I wasn't complaining, Dad, just commenting. How's the soccer team coming, Dyana?"

What could she say, awful? "Fine. The girls seem to be catching on quickly."

"Good," Phillip said. "We'll have to come see them play this season."

Dyana smiled. "Maybe you'd better wait until next season."

Which made Phillip laugh. "You'll do fine."

"She's rough on them," Chad commented. "I watched practice today and she didn't give an inch."

"I'm afraid that's a family trait," Phillip bantered back. "These two ladies are a very stubborn lot."

Darcy poked him. "Be nice."

But he'd been teasing and they all laughed.

"Well." Darcy put the platter of appetizers down and headed for the door. "I'd better get dinner going or we're never going to eat."

Dyana had been looking for an excuse to talk with her sister. She jumped up to follow Darcy inside. "Want some help?"

"Oh, no, you stay here with Chad."

"I'm sure Chad will be fine without me," Dyana remarked dryly.

His smile was pleasant, amused. "Go ahead. We've got all weekend to be together. I'll chat with Phillip."

She glanced at him. The man went from bad to worse. The last thing she had expected was for him to give her *permission* to go with her sister. And his remark about the weekend was practically an announcement. "Gee, thanks."

"You're welcome."

Dyana wanted to slap the grin off his face, but she turned and followed her sister into the house.

"Would get the potato salad out?" Darcy asked when they entered the kitchen.

"No," Dyana answered. "Not yet. Darcy, I want to talk to you."

"Is something wrong?"

How her sister could look so innocent was beyond Dyana, but Darcy's blue eyes were clear and bright. "Yes, something's wrong. I'm your sister. How could you do this to me? How could you betray me like this?"

Still the innocent look. "How have I betrayed you?"

"Darcy, why didn't you tell me that Chad was calling you?"

"He asked me not to."

"I'm your *sister*," Dyana said. "Doesn't that count for anything?"

Darcy went to the refrigerator and got out the potato salad herself. "Of course it counts for something, but Tubbs wanted to surprise you."

"And you didn't want to spoil it?"

"Well, of course not. What's a surprise if it's not a surprise? Dyana, he wants to get back together with you."

She shook her head in frustration. "Darcy, having kids has warped your mind. I'm not nine years old. Some surprises can be spoiled, and I don't know what it is that Chad wants from me, but it's not to get back together."

"He just wants you to get to know him again. He's sorry for what happened between you."

"You're so naïve," Dyana said. "Don't you understand? I went home with him that night. He made love to me."

Her sister had been piling up cups and plates. Darcy turned to look at her for a long time, not saying anything. Then she placed her hand on Dyana's arm and murmured softly, "That doesn't make you a bad person.

Phillip and I made love before we were married."

She sighed. Darcy had missed the point altogether. Turning away, she picked up the potato salad and stirred it. "But you were in love."

"And you're not?"

"I hardly know him. How can I be in love with him?"

"You were in love with him once."

"Darcy, I was a kid. You don't fall in love in high school. At least not forever."

"At one time I would have agreed with that," Darcy said, pulling out a Jell-O mold and frowning at it, "but not anymore. Look at Helen and Troy." They were friends of Phillip's who got married right out of high school. "They were childhood sweethearts."

"They're an exception. This nostalgia thing is cute, but it's not serious."

"There's always an exception. And it's not nostalgia. Personally, I think Tubbs is very much in love with you, and I think you're in love with him. You're just too stubborn to admit it. You're angry because you got up and he was gone."

"Did he tell you that?" Dyana gasped, horrified.

"Is it true?"

"Yes," Dyana grated out.

"Sorry. That was really rotten of him, and no, he didn't tell me. I figured it out when he called. How's the potato salad? Did you taste it?"

Attention diverted momentarily, Dyana took a bite of the concoction. She couldn't help her grimace. "It's a good thing Phillip is smitten with you, Darcy. Obviously the man does not stay with you because of your culinary abilities."

"That bad?"

"You've got to learn how to cook."

"You're not much better, little sister."

"True, but at least I can bake a chocolate cake." Darcy's cakes were the joke of the family. One day, when Mandy had been little, she'd gone to a birthday party. When she'd come home, she'd asked Darcy how come the kid's cake didn't have tunnels in it, like her cakes.

"Just barely."

"Is Phillip cooking the hamburgers tonight? Or are we in danger of a fire?" Once, when Darcy had first been dating Phillip, she had burned up the hamburgers. Dyana had always suspected that they'd been kissing. Chad had been over and they'd had to hose the grill down. Then they'd started a water fight. By the time it was all over, the fire department and the police both had come. But it had been a lot of fun. It had been the start of their intimate relationship. Later that summer she'd discovered he wasn't just a boy but a man, and he'd discovered her womanly curves.

"Actually, Dad is going to cook the hamburgers. Mom got him new barbecue tools and he brought them with him."

Dyana picked up a piece of celery and started to nibble on it. "I'm thinking about going away with Chad for the weekend."

Darcy didn't blink an eye at the lightning-quick change in subject. "Oh? Where to?"

"The Delmarva Peninsula."

"That sounds like fun."

"How do you think Mom and Dad will take it?"

Darcy shrugged. "I'm not sure. They like Tubbs. They always have. And you're certainly beyond the age of parental consent. I doubt they think you're a virgin anymore."

"Parents always think you're a virgin," Dyana sighed. "It's a given."

"That's because they have a hard time dealing with

the sexuality of their children. Believe me, I know. Mandy's only nine and I'm already dreading her first date. Say, what's the decision on the potato salad? Are we going to serve it?"

Dyana glanced down at the bowl. "Sure, why not? We'll tell Chad I made it, and if he can get it down without choking to death, then we'll know for sure that he's in love with me."

Darcy laughed. "And here I thought you were such a sweet person."

Dyana laughed, too. "I am sweet. But I'm also vindictive."

"And afraid?"

For all her nonchalance, Darcy was amazingly perceptive. "Very."

"Love's like that. It's a big step."

"Too big."

"Not really. Not if it's the right person and for the right reasons."

That was the problem. Dyana wasn't certain of Chad's reasons. So far he'd come here and disrupted her life, but he hadn't convinced her of why. Or that it meant anything to him. That it was forever.

"I'm sure you'll work it out," Darcy went on, gathering up the food to take outside. "At least I hope so."

They went out the door. Chad was still sitting in the lawn chair, talking to Phillip. Dyana glanced at him, and for a moment he took her breath away. "So do I," she murmured aloud. "Oh, so do I."

CHAPTER
Six

CHAD ATE SEVERAL helpings of potato salad. So did Phillip. Dyana shrugged when Darcy gave her a curious glance. Obviously it tasted better than she thought. After dinner they had cake with tunnels in it. Chad's parents looked at it a little strangely, but Chad ate it as if he didn't even notice the holes. He seemed more concerned with the fat content than the air molecules, and limited himself to one small bite.

Dyana had no such compunction about calories. She ate the remains of Chad's cake while she helped Darcy clear the table.

"Such steely self-control," she said, returning to sit beside him.

He looked a little regretful. "I have to enjoy everything vicariously," he said, and then amended, smiling at her, "Almost everything."

Darcy giggled. All four parents, thank God, looked a little puzzled. Dyana, feeling her face flame, turned her chair so she could converse easily with the other adults. The subject was changed, the air was no longer charged with innuendo, and she was just beginning to grow comfortable.

Then Mr. Weber said to Chad, "Are you going to be able to get in any crabbing this weekend when you and Dyana go up to Maryland?"

"Probably not," Chad answered. "But one of the guys on the team has a sailboat moored in the Baltimore Inner Harbor. I thought we might stay in Baltimore and give that a try. I'd like to sail down to St. Martin's. Depends on what Dyana wants to do."

"But Dyana can't swim," said Mrs. Kincaid. "I'm not sure she should go out on a boat in the ocean. Dyana, do you think you should go out on a boat in the ocean when you can't swim?"

"It's the Chesapeake Bay, Mother," Dyana's father said. "Only the Chesapeake Bay. You make it sound like the middle of the Pacific in a typhoon."

"But she can't *swim*," said Mrs. Kincaid.

"Don't worry, Martha," said Chad's mother. "Chadwick will take good care of her."

Chadwick? Dyana hadn't heard anyone call him by his full name in years. But she didn't have time to tease him about it. She was too busy digesting the fact that apparently he'd mentioned their trip to both sets of parents. Since she couldn't melt through the wood of the deck Phillip had built, she turned to Chad and whispered, "You told them?"

"Accidentally. We were talking about fishing and I said we were thinking about going to the bay this weekend. I'm sorry," he added. "I realize I've made things awkward for you."

For once he seemed sincere, and he even looked sorry as he gazed across the picnic table at her. Actually, her parents were taking it rather well, if all they were concerned about was her being in a boat on the ocean. Obviously they hadn't figured out that being with Chad on a sunny shore was more dangerous than the middle of the Pacific in a typhoon.

Besides, she remembered, she hadn't actually accepted his invitation yet. Was she really going to refuse to go?

If she was going to say no, now was the time to say it.

She opened her mouth, rounded her lips, took a breath. And *no* didn't come out. Chad, watching her, grinned.

"Too bad you're not fishing on the Atlantic side. You could go after marlin," Chad's father said. "They're a great game fish. Real fighters."

Her own father nodded. "I had one on the hook for hours a couple of years ago. By the time I had him landed, I was exhausted."

Darcy said, "How can you stand to kill something that fights that hard to live?"

Phillip groaned. "My little wildlife activist," he said. "I spend half my time justifying my fishing worms."

"Well, you should," said Darcy, then she turned to her father. "What did you do with the poor fish?"

He looked at her over the top of his glasses. "I cut him loose. He swam away and lived to fight another day." He grinned at her. "How do think you came by your attitude toward hunting and fishing? I haven't brought home a fish in forty years. I always cut them loose."

Chad leaned toward Dyana. "Do you want to be cut loose, too?" he asked.

All she had to say was, "I'm not going." She took another breath, got out the *I*, and closed her mouth with a sigh.

Chad leaned back in his chair and looked entirely too self-satisfied. He hadn't been worried that she'd say no. No woman ever had, she supposed, and what reason would he have to think that she would be the first?

The children were in a neighbor's yard, squabbling over a jar of fireflies. Darcy got to her feet and called their names. "When they start fighting like that, it's time to get them to bed," she announced.

That was a signal. Everyone stood. Mr. Weber knocked his pipe against the stump of a tree and covered the ashes with dirt in the flower bed. Tom Kincaid took his wife's hand.

"Well, good night, folks," said Phillip. "I think I just heard a message to run the bathwater. It's my night to see that the kids wash behind their ears."

Chad had Dyana by the arm, pulling her toward the door. "We have to pack," he said.

Dyana gave a weak smile. "I do have a lot to take care of." Had the man no discretion whatsoever? Next he'd be discussing the sleeping arrangements. But her parents didn't seem to notice, or if they noticed, they didn't seem to care.

"Be careful on that boat," said Dyana's mother hugging her.

"If you get tired of Baltimore, drive over to the Atlantic and bring home the marlin I left behind," said her father.

"Make Dyana wear her seat belt, and don't drive too fast. You know how you are about driving too fast," said Chad's mother, as if they were two little kids going out to cross the street for the first time, instead of a grown man and woman about to spend the weekend together.

Alone.

She knew she was blushing. Damn it. But then, she knew Chad was trying to hook more than a marlin.

Chad's car purred quietly along the streets to the school, where she'd left her trusty little Ford. Why was she allowing herself to be led along like a lamb to the slaughter? She'd lost all her ability to reason. He'd left her twice, after they'd made love, and it hadn't seemed to trouble him at all. He wasn't bothered by leaving her, and he wasn't bothered by her anguish over it. She was being stupid, really stupid, setting herself up to be hurt and not even trying to do anything about it.

When Chad pulled up in front of the school, he shut off the engine and turned toward her. "Do you have time to talk for a minute?"

Those were the first words either of them had said on the entire drive.

"About what?"

"I just want to apologize again for making you feel uncomfortable with your parents. I didn't mean to embarrass you. I didn't intend to tell our parents we were going away together for the weekend. But I'm not accustomed to doing anything I need to conceal, so when Dad mentioned fishing, it just popped out."

"It's all right. I understand." She understood she had just decided to spend a weekend alone with the most dangerous man in the Western Hemisphere.

"I know I smooth-talked you into this trip," Chad went on. "You didn't really agree to go. I just assumed you would, and I'm beginning to feel guilty about it. I want you to know that you can back out at any time."

She remembered his self-satisfied smile back at Darcy's house, when she'd tried to say no and her subconscious had stopped her.

"All right," she said. "I'm backing out." Then she was immediately sorry. She wanted to go. Very much. She shrugged before he could react. "I'm kidding. I'm going. What woman could turn down a weekend with you?"

"You could," he said quietly, and she knew he meant it.

"You could have smooth-talked me all day," she told

him. "If I hadn't wanted to go, it wouldn't have worked."

He smiled. "You're immune to my charm."

"What charm?"

That made him laugh. "That's right. Put me in my place. Just leave the doghouse door open so I can get a little fresh air." His expression grew serious again. "Dyana, it's so important for us to get away together and get to know each other again. The rest of our lives depend on it."

She looked away from him, across the moonlit trees toward the horizon. "We're not seventeen, Chad. We can't build on what we thought we had. That's gone now."

"Is it?" he asked.

"When we thought we loved each other, we were children. It wasn't love, it was lust. And we're not children anymore. We've changed."

"It felt like love to me then," said Chad. "And looking back on it, it still feels like love. Seventeen or seventy. It's the same thing."

She looked at him. "It's not," she said sharply. "If you kept your hands off me for ten minutes and gave your hormones a rest, you'd find that out."

"All right, then," he said. "Come to Baltimore with me, and I won't touch you."

"Damn straight," she said irritably, wondering why in hell she was making a stupid deal like that.

He laughed again. "You know something, Dyana Kincaid? I think I've met my match. I never know exactly what I'm going to get from you." He pulled a velvet jewelry box from his pocket. "Here," he said, handing it to her. "I brought you something. I wanted to get you alone to give it to you."

She glanced down at the dainty box, not quite sure how to react. Accepting presents from him was like . . .

selling herself. Particularly since she was absolutely certain that she was just another woman in his collection. He had never been serious. He was probably incapable of it. He'd proven that once before—but, like she'd told him, they'd been children the first time they'd made love. That was lust. And then his lust took him to Jeannie Williamson and left Dyana Kincaid embarrassed, wounded, insecure, and unhappy.

But he'd been only seventeen. Could men change?

She looked at the box again. "For me?" she said.

He moved closer to her and put his arm across the back of the seat to let his hand rest lightly on her dark curls. "I hope you like it," he said.

"What is it?" Her hands felt trembly. She grasped the box tightly.

"Why don't you open it and find out?"

"I shouldn't be taking presents from you, Chad." Oh, God. He thought he could buy her.

"You don't even know what it is."

"Nevertheless."

"Nevertheless what? Do I have leprosy?"

"That's not the point, and you know it."

He nodded. "I know. Just look at it, okay? No strings attached. You don't owe me anything."

"There is no such thing as 'no strings attached,'" she said, trying to explain.

He brushed at the curls around her face. "Decide that after you open it," he suggested persuasively.

He was so difficult to argue with. With a sigh she gave up and opened the box. Nestled inside the dark velvet was a long gold chain with a small, delicate pink quartz crystal attached to it. The chain alone had to be terribly expensive, and the stone was spectacularly flawless.

"It's beautiful," she murmured as it caught the light from passing cars and flashed it back at them.

"I thought it was kind of appropriate, considering our history with quartz."

"Chad, I—" If he was trying to buy her, he was using sentiment as the currency, and not just money. She looked at the quartz and remembered the first time they'd made love. So young. So frightened by their passion. And made so angry by their fear that they had never recovered.

He let his hand slip off her hair to caress her neck. "Will you wear it for me?" he asked, his voice low and infinitely tender.

"Oh, Chad, I don't think—"

But he wasn't taking no for an answer. Before she could voice a protest, he took the chain from her and fastened it around her neck. "Just call it a peace offering from long ago."

Ten years, to be exact. He touched the crystal. It fell just below the tops of her breasts and nestled there between them, as personal as the touch of his finger.

She took his hand in both of hers to move it away from her. Her heart was beating so rapidly, she thought it must be visible with every light that flashed. "I don't know what to say."

He let the hand she'd moved caress her thigh. "How about just plain thank you?"

She laughed and broke the spell. "Thank you," she said.

He straightened in the seat. "See you tomorrow?"

Dyana knew he was asking if she really intended to go with him to Baltimore? She hesitated for just an instant and then said, "Yes."

She wanted to go with him. All her fears couldn't brush away her desire. She wanted to spend time alone with him, to see if perhaps she was wrong, if maybe she could make him forget all those other women in all those years they'd been apart. Perhaps she *was* being set up, but she was also being handed an opportunity, and she didn't intend to pass it up.

He relaxed beside her, as if all his muscles had been stretched taut and then released. "Good. I'm glad. Dyana . . ." His voice was husky and he tilted her chin so that she was looking into his incredible, dark, desiring eyes. "This is the weekend we're going to fall in love again."

The low, soft words frightened her almost as much as his touch, feathering along her jaw. She licked her lips nervously. "You know something, Chad Weber?" she asked, her voice low, to match his. "I think I've met my match."

"We could be quite a pair," he said. "If we give us a chance." His fingers dipped inside her collar and moved lightly across the naked skin under her shirt.

She couldn't stand it. "I thought you weren't going to touch me," she said.

"I meant this weekend."

"It's already Friday." She opened the door. "You're supposed to start now."

"It's only eleven-thirty. I don't start not touching you until midnight."

"I can't stay here until midnight. I have to go."

He moved his hands and released her. "I'll follow you home."

She glanced at her car, sitting alone in the parking lot. "That's not necessary. I'll be fine."

"I insist." He sounded as if he would brook no opposition.

It was all that football, Dyana thought. He was too accustomed to winning. "It's not too far, and besides, nobody would come into my apartment. I have an attack cat on the premises." If you could call shy little Josie an attack cat.

"Don't bother to argue, Dyana. It won't do you any good."

Even though she was a little annoyed at being so peremptorily ordered around, it was sort of a relief that Chad insisted. She hated to admit it, but sometimes she was uneasy about returning to her apartment late at night. It was so secluded, and there was so much crime in cities.

"Fine," she agreed, then paused. "Are we really going on a boat way out in the ocean?"

He leaned across the seat and placed his hand on hers. "Don't worry. If the boat sinks, I'll be there to save you."

Now, why didn't that give her a feeling of security? "Right," she said. "I'll see you tomorrow."

"I'll pick you up after soccer practice."

"I'll be ready." She glanced at him one last time before she got in her car and drove off, wondering all over again why she was doing something so ludicrously outside her own self-interest as a weekend trip with the Gridiron Idol of the Universe. She'd never gone away with a man before. Hell, she'd only made love with two other men. One had been her fiancé; the other a silly college experience, when she'd tried to prove to herself that she wasn't abnormal because she didn't sleep around. Why was she going away with Chad? And why now? For old times' sake? She ought to be fighting that irresistible physical attraction. She could never make him love her. He was too worldy and she was too much the small-town high school counselor. They had nothing in common, except a long-ago puppy love. She knew she was going to be hurt again, and she knew she was going to be very, very sorry she'd ever seen Chad at that reunion.

By the time they left the next afternoon, she was terribly tired. She'd spent most of the night tossing and turning and trying to sort out her feelings from her fears. The school day was long and tiring, and all day long, between students who came to her with problems, she'd questioned the wisdom of going away with Chad. But when he'd come for her, she'd followed him as blithely as if she hadn't a question in her heart, onto the plane in Chicago and off it again in Baltimore.

But being terribly tired did nothing to keep her from being terribly nervous—about Chad, about his intentions, and about her own. She hadn't intended to make love either time they had done it. She had been swept away by passion, and she didn't want to have that happen to her again. It was just that the touch of his hands on her skin, the fire of his kisses, the heat of his breath, and the heavy, excited thud of his heart against her own aroused her beyond bearing. She needed to keep something physically between them: tables, walls, locked doors, and big, noisy crowds in public places.

Cleopatra had been stupid. She should have headed south as soon as Marc Antony walked through the door of the palace. But Dyana supposed no empress ever thought of herself as vulnerable.

Dyana was no empress. She knew she was vulnerable and felt it acutely. She had showered after soccer practice and changed into a soft turquoise sleeveless dress made of a T-shirt knit. It clung to her as if she were its only security, and exposed more of her figure than she felt comfortable showing to the world. Chad had mentioned it appreciatively, and while she was glad he approved, she was beginning to wish she'd left it in the closet and worn jeans, like Chad.

She looked at Chad as he wheeled the rental car expertly into the drive of a small hotel in Baltimore's Inner Harbor area. He was just so damn sexy, it was a shame —all that beautiful hair just waiting for the touch of her fingers. The clean, firm line of his jaw underscoring his thin, flexible, very talented lips. Oh, what he could do to her with those lips! It didn't bear thinking about.

She said quickly, before the doorman could open her car door, "I'll pay my own hotel bill. I don't want to feel like a kept woman." Then she got out before Chad could say a word.

He caught up with her in the lobby. "Whatever makes you comfortable," he said. "That's what I want."

She had expected derision and opposition and was surprised by the gentleness of his tone. At the check-in desk he surprised her again.

"Chad Weber and Dyana Kincaid," he said. "We have reservations."

The clerk looked at them knowingly, handed Chad a form to complete, and asked for his credit card.

Chad pushed the form toward Dyana and smiled. "Miss Kincaid can put her room on her own expense account," he said to the clerk. "Why don't you let me have another check-in sheet?"

Immediately the clerk's attitude toward Dyana changed. Obviously, from the way he treated her now, he thought she was a business traveler, instead of half of a weekend couple seeking an assignation. He took two keys off the board behind him.

Dyana, feeling much less conspicuous, smiled at Chad gratefully. The clerk, seeing the smile, looked confused, thought a minute, and exchanged the keys in his hand for two others, which he handed to the bellboy who handled their bags.

Then he said hesitantly, "Mr. Weber?"

Chad paused.

The clerk was flushed to the roots of his hair. He held a pad and ballpoint pen clutched close to his skinny chest. "I don't want to intrude on your privacy," he said, "but could I have your autograph?" He stuck the pad out convulsively, as if his arms had a mind of their own, and he was obviously so impressed by the presence of football royalty that he was shaking with the effects of his presumptuous request.

Chad took the pad. "Sure," he said. "I don't mind a bit." Smiling, he handed the signed paper to the clerk, who then extended it to Dyana.

"Please, would you mind signing it, too?" he said. "I'm not sure who you are, but I'm sure you're somebody because you're with Mr. Weber, and from L.A., and you're probably in the movies. At least"—he was confused now but he took a deep breath and forged on—"you *look* like you're in the movies, so please?"

"Go ahead," said Chad, grinning. "I guess he's recognized us both."

Dyana gave Chad a scalding glare. "I'm not anybody you'd be interested in," she assured the clerk. "You really don't want my signature."

"Yes, I do," affirmed the clerk, emboldened by Chad's reaction to his request. "I *know* you're in the movies." He added, "That's a really good disguise. Almost no one would know who you are."

"Go ahead, darling," said Chad. "You don't want him to think movie stars are stuck-up, do you?" He took the pad and shoved it into Dyana's hands. "She's going to sign with her real name, not her stage name. It's an autograph that will be tremendously valuable someday. Worth much more than mine."

"Chad, for goodness sake!" said Dyana. But she signed. She couldn't afford not to—she didn't want the man to think movie stars were stuck-up. Besides, she and Chad had already made a scene. A crowd had gathered, and most of them were fumbling in their pockets and purses for papers and pens. "Oh, my," she murmured, looking up.

Chad was taking papers, right and left, and signing autographs as fast as he could write. As he finished, he handed them to Dyana, who stood rooted to the spot.

"Chad!" she said. "This is misrepresentation."

He didn't even look up. "Better get to signing, dear," he said. "If you want to get through in time for dinner." He stopped once and fished in his pocket for a twenty-dollar bill, which he gave to the bellboy. "While we finish here, would you take our luggage to our rooms and wait there until we come?"

"Yes, sir," said the bellboy. "If you'll just autograph that twenty."

"Sure," said Chad. "What's your name?"

"Walter Robertson."

Chad wrote, "To Walter Robertson, with best wishes from Chad Weber" and young Walter handed the bill to Dyana. With a sigh she added her name to Chad's. Walter examined it proudly. "I'm gonna frame this," he said. "I'm gonna hang it right in my mom's living room, next to Arnold Palmer and Paul Newman. I got a collection."

In a few minutes Chad began to edge toward the elevator. As he reached it, still autographing scraps of paper, dollar bills, cigarette packages, and paper shopping bags, he punched the call button. It arrived, and he waited until the last second, shoved Dyana in as the doors began to close, and said through the narrowing space, "Thanks, folks. We'll see you later."

The elevator stopped on the fourth floor. The bellboy waited at the end of a long hall.

"Is this my room?" Dyana asked. It was huge and luxurious, and instead of the usual two double beds, it had a king-size bed with a designer spread, a matching love seat, and two comfortable chairs.

"Yes, ma'am," he said. He took another twenty from Chad's outstretched hand, gave him the keys, and faded around a corner.

"Where are you staying?" Dyana asked. Then she

saw the open door connecting her room with the one next to it.

Chad saw the look in her eye. "I didn't have a thing to do with it," he protested.

"And I'm a movie star, you liar."

"I didn't, I swear. You saw the clerk pick those two keys off the shelf yourself."

"What did you give him to do it?" she asked. "Get out of here." She had *known* she was being set up! How could she think a man like Chad Weber, who had women all over the nation falling at his feet, would take an interest in a woman who wouldn't make love whenever he wanted to? And even if she refused to welcome him into her arms, who in the world would ever believe they slept in separate beds and never saw each other from night till morning? Nobody!

But she really couldn't be too angry. Chad really hadn't had anything to do with the room assignments. The clerk had seen them together and made the wrong assumption. Or maybe, she thought ruefully, he had made the right assumption. She didn't know what she wanted to have happen herself. Maybe they would wind up in the same bed. Chad might have promised not to touch her, but she hadn't made any such promise to him.

Chad walked into the next room, and she pushed the door shut with a decisive click. In a minute there came a tentative knock.

"Hey, lady?" Chad said.

"What?"

"I don't know who you are, but I know you're somebody, and I want to take you to dinner because I'm faint with hunger."

She giggled and opened the door. He was leaning against the jamb, trying to look weak.

"Where are we going to go?" she asked, looking past

him into his room. It was much smaller, furnished with
the conventional two double beds, which took up most
of the floor space.

"I know whom that clerk was trying to impress," said
Chad. "And it wasn't me." He walked past her and
opened the curtains over a window that showed a pano-
ramic view of the Inner Harbor. It was just dark outside,
and across a little spit of water that was full of boats
docked for the night there were two large buildings on a
pier, their lights beginning to flame.

"See that?" he said. "That's Harbor Place. It's like a
bazaar, full of interesting things—serapes from Mex-
ico, saris from India, crystal from Ireland, and food
from everywhere—including the Chesapeake Bay. I
thought we'd wander around in there till we eat our-
selves into a stupor, spend all our money, and ruin our
arches from too much walking. How about it?"

She ducked under his arm to look. The pier was
crowded with people. She could hear laughter and an
excited mumble of voices, but she didn't think it came
from outside. It sounded like a party next door.

"Can we go down there without getting mobbed?"
she asked, mindful of the unsettling scene in the lobby.

"I don't know," said Chad. "I can't guarantee anything." He circled her with his arm and she let herself
settle back against him.

"I thought you promised not to touch me," she said.

"I did?" he said. "I meant I promised not to make
love to you again until you are ready for it. I never
promised not to touch you." He smoothed the soft curls
from her neck and lowered his head to kiss her behind
the ear.

"Yes, you did," she said. She knew she should pull
away from him. She shouldn't let him get so close—
she turned into putty every time he touched her, and she
really needed time to think about her feelings for him

without the additional complication of sex. But will was no match for desire. She turned in his arms and lifted her face to his. His hands at her waist melted into her, urging her closer. His kiss, hard and urgent, demanded a response. She wrapped her arms around him eagerly to give him what he wanted.

There was a sudden blaze of light, and Chad jerked away from her convulsively. Across the street was a photographer with a telephoto lens pointed at their window.

"Damn!" Chad said, and angrily yanked the curtains closed.

Dyana ran her fingers through her hair and shuddered. "Is it always like this for you?" she asked. "Do they follow you everywhere and never let you have a minute's peace?"

"It's not always this bad," he said unhappily. "Dyana, don't judge my life by this. Usually it isn't this bad—people are pretty nice most of the time. Like that clerk downstairs."

"How can you do it?" she asked, wondering. "I think it would drive me crazy."

"It does, a little," he admitted. "At first. But pretty soon you don't even notice it." He sat on the end of the bed and pulled her down beside him. "You want to try to go out? It isn't much worse than being in the circus. I just try to remember I'm only the lion tamer and not the star of the whole show."

"Or Cleopatra floating on her barge down the Nile, off to improve her collection of asps," said Dyana, feeling desperate. She was about to add notoriety to the insecurity, inadequacy and shameless lack of self-control in the already crowded area of her brain where she stored her guilt.

"Cleopatra?" asked Chad.

"Never mind. It's a private joke between me and myself. Senseless to anybody listening into my mind."

"Let me decide for myself."

"What, and confuse you when I need you for protection out in that crowd?" She got to her feet and tugged at his hand. "Come on. Let's go. You bring the whip and I'll bring the chair."

She marched to the door and opened it, ready to party through the night. That was when she discovered that the noise she'd thought had come from next door was really a crowd of celebrity seekers in the hall, waiting for Chad. They surged forward, waving papers, flashing instant cameras, shouting his name.

She gasped and retreated. Chad, looking grim, took her hand and opened the door again. "Look pleased to see them, or every paper in the nation will say you're a snob," he warned.

So she fixed a smile to her face and let him lead her through the mob to the pier outside. Cameras flashed and whirred. People shouted questions. There was even a crew from one of the TV stations, and Chad had to stop to predict the fortunes of the Crusaders for the fall season. He sounded perfectly relaxed and full of good spirits.

Dyana had never in her life felt so out of place.

CHAPTER
Seven

ONCE THEY WERE actually onto the pier, with hundreds of people around them, the requests for autographs slowed to a trickle. But the stares and excited murmurs didn't. Dyana clutched Chad's hand tightly, wondering how long it had taken him to become accustomed to such exposure. He never appeared upset or annoyed by it. He just smiled and nodded at his fans and continued about his business.

Every woman on the pier was watching Chad. Dyana couldn't blame them. She wanted to look at him herself. His jeans were tight across his long thighs, and the short-sleeved knit shirt outlined his broad shoulders and revealed every clean, well-developed muscle in his arms. He really was the sexiest man Dyana had ever seen. And judging from the nudges and whispers around them, he was probably the sexiest man any woman had ever seen. It wasn't just the way he looked, either, though that would have been enough. It was the way he moved. He guided Dyana through the crowd with the grace and coordination that had made him so successful at avoiding tacklers that he was the highest-scoring end in the history of the NFL. That's why he had won the Lamborghini and the Mercedes, and as far as Dyana was concerned, they should have given him a couple of palaces and a kingdom to go with the cars.

There was a magician just outside the door of the first building who was claiming to be able to make a sailboat disappear. "Not as big as the Statue of Liberty, folks," he told a group assembling on the pier in front of him, "but just as hard to do away with."

He had a loudspeaker set up. Many of the people who had been following Chad and Dyana turned away to watch.

Chad grinned. "See?" he said. "The public is fickle. One minute you're famous, and the next minute some guy comes along with a better act and you're history."

"Let's get inside," Dyana suggested, "before somebody who likes history comes along." She pushed through the door and he followed.

Just to her right was a burger stand. Next to it was a place that sold ice cream and waffles. Dyana swerved into it as if she were on automatic pilot. Chad pulled her back into the aisle.

"Can't have dessert before you have dinner," he said.

"There's dinner everywhere," Dyana told him. "Look around. We can eat anything." There were French restaurants, seafood shops, burger palaces, oyster bars. Suddenly she was ravenously hungry. "Let's stop at the first one we come to."

"Do you like boiled crab?"

"I don't know," she confessed. "I've never had any."

"Well, you're in for a juicy, messy treat."

She followed him out the side door to a waterside table under a big sign that read MISS SUSIE'S. As they passed the waiter's stand Chad snaked out a hand and picked up a bumper sticker. "Here's something for your car," he said, handing it to her.

Dyana looked at it. It said, in two-inch red letters: I
GOT THE CRABS AT MISS SUSIE'S PLACE.

"Just the thing to impress the school board in my
district," she said. "Not to mention the kids I counsel.
Put it back."

Chad chuckled and folded it into his shirt pocket.

They sat at a long picnic table covered with sheets of
brown wrapping paper. When they had been joined by
three other couples, a waiter came along with the menu.
There were only four items on it: deviled crab, crab-
cake sandwiches, crab-cake platters, and boiled crab.

"Want some beer?" asked Chad, and when she nodded, he ordered a full pitcher of beer and the boiled crab
special: "All you can eat—$10.95."

In a few minutes the waiter brought the crabs,
heaped high on a tin tray; two glasses of water; the
pitcher of beer; a roll of paper towels; two plastic bibs; a
tub of melted butter; and two wooden mallets. Dyana
looked at the strange collection dubiously.

"Tie on a bib," Chad instructed, "then just grab a
crab and whang away at it with that mallet."

Gingerly she picked a crab off the plate and laid it on
the paper in front of her. "Whang away?"

"Yep." He was whanging already. He pulled a bit of
meat out of a claw, dipped it in the butter, and put it in
her mouth. "This is what you get as a reward for all the
work."

It was delicious. "Give me another bite," Dyana
said.

He put another piece in her mouth, then said,
"There's a limit to my generosity. Get some of your
own."

She tapped the crab lightly with the mallet. Nothing
happened. She hit it a little harder. It bounced but didn't
crack. She gave a mighty whack and flattened it sending
bits of shell, meat, and juice splashing for two yards.

Chad laughed out loud.

"My technique isn't too good," she said. She glanced around her to see if anyone had noticed. The whole restaurant was looking at her.

"Here, honey," he said. "Let me do one for you." He took a crab off the heap and gave it a few strategic taps with the mallet. It cracked in half a dozen places and he pulled the meat out for her. "There you go. Want me to do another one?"

She shook her head. "I have to do it for myself. I can't depend on having you around every time I want to crack a crab."

He gave her a smoky look that curled her toes. "Oh, I think you probably can."

She looked at him helplessly, "Chad . . ."

"Get used to it," he told her. "I may not always be in arm's reach—I do have to work for a living—but I'll always be available if you need me. And most of the time when you want me."

"Impossible," she said involuntarily.

"It's that expectation I am trying to change," Chad said.

"We don't lead the same kinds of lives."

"You can come lead mine with me."

"What if I don't want to? I don't think I could live with the gawking crowds, the women coming on to you constantly, and the lack of privacy. Besides, I like my job."

"You like your job, but you love me," said Chad with quiet assurance. "You'll realize that sooner or later. We can work out a way to deal with the rest of it."

He was so sure of himself, so accustomed to getting what he wanted. He just decided the way he wanted things to be—and presto! the world bowed to his command.

But Dyana wasn't sure she could become accustomed

to his lifestyle. She wasn't sure yet that she wanted to, and even if she found that she did, she wasn't sure she could. She thought she might finally get used to the constant publicity and lack of privacy, if she worked at it hard enough. But she knew she would always feel worried and inadequate about combating the hordes of beautiful women who threw themselves at Chad. He was only human. Women could turn down that sort of thing, but men were different.

And Chad had sampled plenty of women in the past —she'd seen their pictures in the newspapers and heard the rumors of their activities. She remembered one in particular, which had appeared about a year ago: "Stacy Carleton, star of the hit television series *Life in the Fast Lane*, indicated that glamour-boy escort Chad Weber might be the father of the baby she expects in May."

Dyana had never heard any more about it, but whether it was true or not, that sort of publicity was sure to continue concerning a man as much in the public eye as Chad.

She sighed, and he examined her keenly.

"Yes?" he asked.

"I was just reflecting that you're a hard guy to resist," she said.

"It will soon be impossible," he said, standing and reaching for her hand. "I have just begun to fight."

The night was fully dark now, and the lights of the city reflected off the still water of the harbor. The sailboats moored close to the dock were beautiful, sleek and long and clean-lined.

"Which one is your friend's boat?" she asked. "I'd like to see it."

"Down this way," he said, leading her away from Harbor Place. "Are you sure you wouldn't rather go shopping?"

She looked over her shoulder. "I'd like to get away from the crowds. I feel a little closed in."

"You'll get used to it," he predicted.

She didn't know whether to laugh or not. "Don't you ever feel that you're just a tad arrogant, Chad?"

He grinned down at her, the same glorious, lopsided grin that made every woman in the nation swoon whenever he was interviewed on TV. "It crosses my mind occasionally. I try to ignore it."

He laced his fingers through hers and drew her closer to him. The ballerina-length skirt of her dress swirled close to her legs. It was so thin, she could feel the seam of his jeans as he pressed against her. Instinctively she pulled away. She could feel people watching them.

He let her put a little distance between them but didn't release her hand. "I don't think I can wait too much longer for a kiss."

"You are not going to kiss me out here in public, surrounded by reporters and gossip columnists and photographers with telephoto lenses!" But she could feel the heat from his long body, could remember with a stirring inside her how it felt to be crushed against his chest and have his lips devouring her. The memory of it laced through her almost painfully and made her long to have it happen again. The danger to her came from herself, not from Chad.

"We'll find a dark corner on this dock somewhere," he promised. "If I let you go too long without attention, you might forget you're supposed to be learning to love me again."

She only wished she could forget. Every atom in her body was in line and waiting for marching orders. All she had to do was let go, just a little bit. She was fighting for what scant self-restraint she had, and her slim control over herself was most disturbing. He knew exactly what he was doing to her, she was sure. He knew that her physical reaction to him was just as inevitable as the sun rising in the east. How hard would a man work to keep a love that was so easy to get? She was afraid she knew the answer to that—she'd seen it on the evening news when Chad appeared, never accompanied by the same woman twice.

He led her around the corner of a dock house, which housed the ropes and supplies the dock master used. He crouched in its shadow and pulled Dyana down beside him. Behind them, seemingly far away, they could hear the echo of footsteps on the wooden pier.

"No one can see us here, Dyana," said Chad. He cupped her head gently in his hands and turned her face to his. Their mouths touched softly. Then he smoothed at her bottom lip with the tip of his tongue, so lightly that she could barely feel it, and she leaned into his arms, yearning for him. His mouth locked on to hers hungrily and his hands roamed over her shoulders, to her waist, skimmed down her hips, and then back again to support the weight of her breasts in his palms. Her nipples beaded hard against his fingers, and he rubbed across them with his thumbs. He leaned against the dock house and pulled her across his lap, and she could feel the hardness of him pressing into her ribs.

The footsteps she'd heard became a roar instead of an echo. A clear voice rang out, "I think he's over here." A cone of light bobbed past the dock house, and Chad swore under his breath and jumped to his feet. "Stay down," he whispered to Dyana. He didn't need to tell her. Nothing in the world could have induced her to reveal herself.

"Hey, Chad," yelled the man with the light, "how about an interview?"

Chad stepped into full view. "How about if you come around to the hotel lobby in the morning and talk to me then? I'd like a little privacy tonight."

"How about you bring out that woman we've seen you with all day? Our sources tell us she's an important Hollywood VIP."

Chad was irritated, and to his everlasting regret it sounded in his tone. "Your sources are wrong. I don't want to talk to you tonight."

Suddenly the night was bright with the glow of a camcorder light. "Think you're too good to talk to your fans, now that you're the highest-paid star in the history of the NFL?"

"Holy cow!" Dyana murmured. Things were getting out of hand. There was the sound of a slight scuffle. Dyana peeked around the corner of the dock house, and a reporter with a camcorder was trying to get around Chad.

"Get away from there!" Chad said.

"It's a public pier," announced the reporter, and he stepped behind the dock house with the camcorder and shined its light on Dyana.

Chad was in trouble. One of the other men was rubbing his wrist and making noises about assault.

So much for remaining hidden. Dyana knew she had to say something to defuse the situation. Unfortunately, what she produced was "Don't shoot, Warden! I'll give myself up!"

The man stopped rubbing his wrist and stuck a microphone in her face. "What's your name, lady?"

"Dyana Kincaid."

"I understand you work in Hollywood."

She shook her head and stepped in front of Chad. "I work at the Meadows High School in Rolling Meadows, Illinois, on the school counseling staff. I have never been to Hollywood, and as a matter of fact, I've never been to Baltimore before tonight. You'll have to forgive Chad if he's a little upset. The crowds around him made me feel a little nervous, so he was just trying to keep me out of the limelight."

"So you're neurotic about crowds?" said the reporter belligerently, trying to lure either Chad or Dyana into a newsworthy rage. "Have a phobia about them?"

Behind her, Chad growled. She put out a hand to quiet him.

"Now, now, let's maintain our dignity, boys and girls," she said in the same bantering tone she used with unruly seventh-graders. "I'm about as phobic as you'd be if I were on the other side of that microphone and you were standing here getting the third degree with that light in your eyes."

Several of the reporters laughed. "Yeah," said one. "Leave her alone, Sandy. Hey, Miss Kincaid, how did you and Chad, here, meet?"

"He put sand in my hair when we were in kindergarten, and I hit him with my shovel. The teacher made us stand in the corner together, and we've been friends ever since."

"And he was your first love, right?"

And her last, she was afraid. She was searching for a noncommittal answer when Chad stepped in front of her and back into the light.

"Give me a break, folks, and let us go. I have to be back in L.A. on Monday, and I don't get a lot of time to relax."

"Sure," said the man with the camcorder. "We got what we came for."

"Not quite," said Sandy. "How are the Crusaders going to do this year?"

"We're going all the way to the Super Bowl."

The man with the camcorder was disappointed. "Aw, all the teams sweet-talk us like that. Can you give us a reason to think you're right?"

"Well," said Chad, considering carefully. "We've

certainly got the talent. Our quarterback is one of the all-time greats; our line is heavy and fast; and we certainly have the depth to cover us in case we have any injuries. So that's my prediction, made in all confidence: We're going to the Super Bowl." He extended his hands, palms up, in a plea. "Now, how about it, guys? Can I have the rest of the night off?"

He waited until they were safely off the pier, then he turned to Dyana and said plaintively, "Geez."

She chuckled. "The burdens of greatness getting to you, superstar?"

He slipped an arm around her waist and nuzzled a quick kiss onto her hair. "You sure handled that great. I didn't know you had it in you."

"I thought that Sandy person was about to have you hauled away for assault. What got into you?" She snuggled against his side, enjoying the closeness of him. Away on the other side of the pier, the crowds were still partying at Harbor Place. Chad pulled her a little closer, and they began to amble in the direction of the hotel.

"You were so upset about the people staring at us," he explained. "I didn't want you to be any more nervous. Besides, how can I convince you to marry me if I can't get you alone?"

She pulled completely away. "If that's why you risked a jail term, you shouldn't have done it. I am not going to marry you, and I wish you'd quit saying that."

To her surprise he agreed. "Okay. I won't mention it again tonight, if you'll come back here and let me put my arm around you, where it belongs."

"That's not where it belongs, but I'll come back." She let him put his arm around her shoulders, and she leaned against him as they walked. "We never did find that boat."

"We'll find it in the morning," he said. "And go for an all-day cruise, far away from the madding crowds."

"What if they get in their own boats and follow us?"
She looked up.

His face, barely outlined by moonlight, was so close
to hers that it made her breathless. "We'll mine the harbor," he said softly, touching her lips with a gentle
finger. "I never did get to finish that kiss, did I?"

"Maybe you should do that," Dyana whispered.

"Maybe I will," said Chad. "Let's go back to the
hotel so we don't have to worry about somebody walking past." He took her hand and headed rapidly down
the street in front of them. Chad's long strides covered
the ground quickly. Dyana was taking two steps to his
one.

"I can't breathe," Dyana panted. "My side hurts.
Slow down."

He stopped immediately until she stopped panting.

"I can't say you're out of shape, exactly," he said,
looking at the dress that clung so becomingly to her
curves. "But is wouldn't hurt you to do wind sprints."

"I don't know what those are, and I hate the sound of
them," Dyana said, setting a more comfortable pace.
"Moderation in all things, speed most of all."

"Moderation is for unexciting people," said Chad.
"People who are afraid to get anything done. The me-
diocre." He urged her into a faster walk and let his hand
slide down to rest on one slim hip. "Think what's waiting for us when we get back."

Dyana thought about it—had been thinking about it
since they'd left their rooms at the beginning of the evening. She wanted Chad so badly that she didn't think
she could stand it. Her desire was even stronger than her
insecurity, and she banished it with the burning ferocity
of flames across a field of dry grass.

Chad looked up the street toward the entrance to the
hotel.

"Uh-oh," he said. "What's waiting for us may have

to wait." There was a parade of limousines disgorging people into the lobby.

"Maybe they won't notice us," said Dyana hopefully. The bellboy who had gotten Chad's autograph on the twenty-dollar bill met them just outside the door.

"I've been watching for you," he said. "The whole lobby's full of people waiting to meet you. I thought maybe you'd like to sneak in the back way."

"Your name's Walter, isn't it?" Chad asked.

"Yes, sir," he said.

"Well, Walter, you're a gentleman and a scholar, and I want you to know you won't have to wait for heaven to get your reward," said Chad.

"I figured I wouldn't, sir," Walter said, grinning as he accepted another twenty-dollar tip. "You go on around to the side of the building. There's a service entrance where the kitchen brings in food. I'll meet you there."

"This is incredible," Dyana said, as they fled through the shadows. "I am actually skulking about in alleys to avoid the press. I can't believe it."

"I believe it," said Chad grimly. "Welcome to the life of the rich and famous."

"Is it always this bad?" she asked. "Didn't I ask you that once before?"

"I can't remember if you asked, but I have to say that this is a new low in public curiosity. Or a new high, depending on how you measure it." They reached the door. The bellboy motioned them inside and signaled for them to be quiet.

Once inside their rooms, another surprise greeted them. Chad's room was completely dark, but Dyana's was obviously arranged for an evening spent by lovers. The lights were low, the music soft. A huge bouquet of flowers, compliments of the management, spread perfume through the air, and beside the huge bed were two bottles of good champagne on ice.

Worse, the bed had been turned down, and sitting on one of the pillows was a silver tray full of expensive Swiss chocolates.

Chad sat on the end of the bed. "Well, so much for trying to maintain a low profile."

Dyana whirled to face him. "Are you trying to make me believe you had nothing to do with this?" She gestured angrily around her.

Chad looked at her, a flash of anger in his own eyes. "I am not going to be stupid enough to pretend I don't want you in my bed. I do, and you know it. But I certainly didn't plan this. It looks like a seduction scene out of one of those old Doris Day–Rock Hudson comedies."

"I'm sorry," she said. "I guess if I'd thought about it, I'd have known this isn't exactly your style." She sank down beside him and sighed. "I can't stand the thought of every sports fan in Baltimore reading about our love nest in the papers."

"And they will, too. Somebody has probably already been up here taking pictures of it."

"What?" said Dyana, alarmed. "How could they? You can't just go into somebody's hotel room. I know the manager arranged for this, but he wouldn't let people in here would he?"

"If he was paid enough, he might." Chad sighed. "I don't know what would be worse," he said. "Having the maid come in tomorrow and finding that only one bed had been slept in, or discovering that two beds were used and assuming we've had a fight."

"Oh, God!" Dyana groaned. "I *knew* I should have stayed in Chicago!"

Chad dropped his arm around her neck. "Well, pardner, there's only one thing to do about this."

"What?"

"Have the maid come in and find that no beds have been slept in." He lay back and gazed at the ceiling. "That way she'll figure we've been out all night, and even if she tells the news media, they won't know where we went. Besides, the damn reporters are about to drive me nuts. I don't know about you, but I am verging on insane right now. I may punch out the next guy who asks me a question, even if it's only the way to the john."

"What are we going to do?" she asked. "Sit up all night?"

"We can sneak out of here with our bags and spend the weekend on the boat. Nobody will know where we are. We can take some sheets and towels and blankets and bring them back here on Sunday when we check out."

Dyana lay on her stomach and propped herself up on her elbows. "Don't you think we might look a little conspicuous, carting all that stuff to the pier? It'll probably take four trips."

Chad reached across her for the phone and dialed the bell captain. "I'd like for you to send Walter Robinson up to my room right away."

Dyana chuckled. "What if they get him for theft, trying to escape with the hotel linens?"

Chad hooked his arm around her neck and gave her a quick, succulent kiss. "I'll pay his bail and hire the best lawyer in the country."

After he explained what he wanted and had augmented Walter's enthusiasm with another twenty dollars, Chad picked up his suitcase and Dyana's. "All right, kiddo," he said through the side of his mouth, like Humphrey Bogart, "let's blow da joint."

They sneaked out through the darkened kitchen and took a back alley to the dock.

"The boat's at the end of Pier 7, all the way around to your left," said Chad. "I can't remember the slip number, but her name is *Pretty Baby*."

Each step took them farther away from the crowds of Harbor Place. Dyana looked around her curiously. Some of the boats were enormous. A few of the sailboats were sixty-footers, but by far the largest were those, with double decks, obviously built for ocean cruising. One they passed had a big deck with sliding glass doors that were open to let air into a cabin as luxurious as any living room Dyana had ever seen. The two people in the cabin reclined on a white couch that looked like leather, and Dyana and Chad could see and hear a television news show in progress. There was Chad, in living color, predicting that the Crusaders would go to the Super Bowl, and Dyana was behind him, standing in the door of her hotel room, looking very wide-eyed and taken aback.

Chad nudged Dyana with one of the suitcases. "Come on, let's get out of here before they turn around." He led the way to the end of the pier, where a sleek white *Pretty Baby* was moored stern-first in the slip. He tossed the suitcases into the cockpit, then stepped across the safety line and held out his hand to help Dyana come on board.

"Stay there a minute," he said. He unlocked the hatchway to the cabin, disappeared, and emerged in a minute with a big orange electric cord with which he connected the boat to the shore power outlet. The cabin lights came on immediately.

"There," he said, "that will make us comfortable for the night. Want to come below?"

"Is that what inside is, *below*?" asked Dyana.

"Yep. Ever been on a sailboat?"

"No," she said. "Is where I'm standing"—she gestured to indicate the wheel and the built-in seats along either side of it— "called *above*?"

"It's called the cockpit. Everything else in open air is the deck. Down here is the cabin." He held up his hands to lift her down. "Come on. Don't you want to see what's here?"

She regarded him suspiciously. "Is that where the beds are?"

"Bunks," he corrected. "Don't you trust me?"

"Are you kidding?" she said, but she stepped carefully over the barrier from the cockpit and onto the ladder into the cabin. "Hey," she said when she got a full view, "this is really nice."

Just in front of her to her right was a small, neat galley. Behind it was a table, with a bench built around three sides of it. Across the center aisle from the table was another bench, and across from the kitchen was a desk of sorts, with what looked like a bed extending under the cockpit outside. At the far end of the cabin was a teakwood door.

"Where does the door go?"

"Forward cabin. This is aft."

"Like after."

"Right."

She went to examine the forward cabin. A raised platform covered with baby-blue cushions filled the entire space, forming a slightly triangular compartment that extended to the bow of the boat.

"This is wall-to-wall bed," Dyana said.

"Very convenient," said Chad innocently. "You can't fall out of it."

She cocked her head at him. "Does this door have a lock?"

He grinned. "I said I wouldn't touch you," he told her.

There was a low whistle from the dock. "Hey, Mr.

Weber," said Walter. When they looked out, Walter was standing in the shadows, surrounded by what looked like sacks of garbage.

"That was a quick trip," said Chad. "Is that the bedding?"

"Yes, sir," said Walter. He passed the bags to Chad, who passed them through the hatch to Dyana. "I brought the champagne and the chocolates, too."

"You're a man of initiative, Walter," said Chad, reaching for his wallet. Walter held up a staying hand.

"Never mind that, sir. You've paid me enough."

Chad sounded disbelieving. "Are you sure you're a bellboy, Walter?" he asked. "And not a reporter in disguise? I never saw a bellboy turn down a tip before."

"A tip is one thing, sir," said Walter. "But this is beginning to amount to extortion. Enjoy the weekend. I took all those linens out of your room, and I hung do-not-disturb signs on the doors."

When he was out of earshot, Chad collapsed on one of the benches and groaned. "He hung do-not-disturb signs on the doors. We might as well have stayed there. Now the maids can imagine just as salacious an interlude as their minds can invent, and sell it to every yellow-journalism gossip rag in the country. I ought to make him give me back the entire sixty dollars—and pay me some, besides."

"Never mind," said Dyana. "I think it was inevitable." She pulled linens out of the plastic bags until she uncovered a bottle of champagne. It was still cold. "I'll open this. You get some of those little plastic glasses out of that thing on the wall."

"Bulkhead," said Chad. "Walls are called bulkheads." He watched her twist the wire basket off the champagne cork. "That bottle has been bounced around so much that it will probably explode."

"Probably," agreed Dyana. She wrapped her hands

around the neck of the bottle and pushed upward on the cork with her thumbs.

"You sure seem to know a lot about that, miss," observed Chad. "Where'd you learn it all?"

"While you were learning about salt spray and bulkheads and above and below and things like that," said Dyana complacently, "I was learning to appreciate good champagne."

"A much more useful skill," agreed Chad as Dyana eased the cork out of the bottle with nothing more than a discreet pop and a cloud of vapor.

She splashed the champagne into the two glasses he put in front of her and put one of them to her lips. "And this is good," she said. "Very, very, very good. I guess knocking about with a celebrity is good for something, after all."

Chad lifted his glass and touched it to hers.

"Here's to health, wealth, long life, and a very happy marriage," he said.

Her big eyes were luminous over the top of the glass. "You said you wouldn't bring that up again."

"I said I wouldn't bring it up again on Friday." He pointed at his watch. "It is now Saturday." He took the champagne from her hand and pulled her across his lap.

"Come here," he said softly. "Let me finish that kiss."

CHAPTER
Eight

DYANA LOST HERSELF in pleasure, and time passed un-
noticed. All the world for her was Chad's arms around
her, Chad's hard body close to hers, Chad's mouth cov-
ering hers, his kisses hot and sweet, and his lips demanding sweetness in return. Her arms clung to him; his
hands roamed across her body, under the soft knit, inside her panties to cup her bottom, moving upward to
cup her breasts. Her skin burned wherever he touched
her. Desire blazed a trail through her. She ached with
wanting him, and she knew he wanted her.

And yet, under the passion was the fear that plagued
her: the image of Chad with a hundred other women.
The line began the first time he left her and took himself
to Jeannie Williamson. It continued through the years.
Beauty queens, starlets, heiresses, women of sophisti-
cation and fashion. If they couldn't keep him with their
beauty and their worldliness, what could he possibly see
in her? She hadn't been woman enough to keep him
from Jeannie Williamson. She knew she wasn't enough
to keep him now. Chad had changed so much, required
so much more than he ever had.

This insidious insecurity gradually worked its way into her head, threading through the Eden they had created like a trickle of dirty water. Though she tried not to withdraw from him, Chad felt the change.

"What's the matter, sweetheart?" he asked softly, raising his head to look into her eyes.

"I haven't had enough champagne for this," she said, hoping that the insecurity that haunted her didn't show in her eyes.

He shook his head, annoyed with himself. "And I said I wouldn't push you. I'm sorry."

She twinkled at him. "I'm not. You owe me a kiss."

Chad looked at her gravely. "It was about to turn into more than a kiss. I want to give you a little time to get to know me again. To figure out what it would be like to have to see me on a daily basis. You can't learn that if all you do is make love—you'll be too busy to notice."

"You'd better stay well away from me, then," she said. "I think I've just demonstrated that I'm not responsible for my actions."

He grinned. "Thank God for that." He moved across the cabin and picked up a set of sheets. "Tell you what —you take the wall-to-wall bunk in the forward cabin, and I'll sleep out here. I want to get an early start tomorrow."

She took the bedding from him and moved to the cabin to make up her bed.

"Want me to do that for you?" he asked. "I'm used to it."

"Not enough room for help. I can manage. How early do you want to leave?"

"Just about dawn," he said. "That way we can avoid those damn reporters—maybe. It'll be a while before they start searching the docks for us."

"This is an awfully big boat. Don't you need for me to help you?" She held out her hand. "I'm ready for the covers."

"It's rigged for single-handed sailing." He passed her a soft white wool blanket. "And in any case, I'll use the motor to get out of the anchorage. Sleep till you're ready to get up."

She turned around and examined the cabin. "Are you going to spend the night on that narrow little bunk?"

He laughed. "All by myself. Isn't that a shame? Or I can sleep down there by the captain's desk, or I can collapse this table and make a double bed right here. Want to share it with me?"

"No thanks, Casanova," she said, wishing she had enough nerve to say yes. "Well, sweet dreams."

"Don't I get a good-night kiss?"

"Are you sure that's compatible with your lofty goal?" she said. "What if I forget to get to know you?"

"I'll kiss you quick," he said, and he did, his hands on her shoulders and not touching her anywhere else. It was not at all what she expected, and certainly not what she wanted.

"That wasn't much of a kiss," she complained.

"I'll do a better job when you decide you love me," he said.

"So how will you know that?"

"You will remember to tell me, won't you? Please decide fast." He turned her around and gave her bottom a light pat to urge her into the bunk. "I don't know how much longer I can continue to be this virtuous. Hey," he said when she closed the door, "better crack that so some cool air can get back there."

So she left the door a little ajar. She could hear him moving around. He wasn't the macho, egotistical man she'd seen at the class reunion. She was beginning to understand that that was a posture he took because it was expected of him. He really was the Tubbs she used to know—and love. All the banter and fun was still there. And so was the quiet consideration. Just chunky Tubbs grown into a tall, handsome, gorgeous man who was as sweet as he'd ever been.

But there was a serious side to him that he hadn't shown as a boy. A willingness to set goals, to work for results, to wait for what he wanted.

He wanted Dyana. He said so. She was willing to believe that; she was also willing to believe he didn't want to hurt her. But what about all those other damn women? Millions and millions and millions of them, clamoring at his door, clutching at his sleeve, kissing him every time they got a chance. And while he said he loved her, he *was* only human. Could any human resist that constant adulation?

She found herself wishing Chad was still Tubbs, and had grown into a slightly stocky, moderately successful insurance salesman or something. Then all those hordes of women wouldn't have the inclination to chase him so, and they'd never find out about the unique, wonderful man he really was. And *he* wouldn't be tempted to stray.

Dyana sighed. She was sure she wouldn't be able to sleep. She had too much to think about. But the swinging of the boat against its mooring lines and the rhythmic slap of the waves against its hull were as soothing as a lullaby, and she woke the next morning to the steady churning of the engine as Chad guided the boat out of the anchorage.

She had slept with no clothes on. She looked at yesterday's underwear with distaste. Her clean clothes were somewhere in the forward cabin. She slipped the knit dress over his head and padded barefoot up the ladder to join Chad in the cockpit.

"Hi, sleepyhead," he said. "How about a kiss?"

She obliged. "Why am I a sleepyhead?" she asked, pointing to the left of the boat. "If I am not terribly mistaken, that pink glow on the horizon means that the sun is just now rising." She looked around—the shore was far away, practically out of sight. "Where are we, anyway?"

"Heading for the Kent Island Narrows. Come here. Take the helm and let me show you how to steer this thing."

She backed away. "If that means using that wheel and doing what you're doing, no thanks. I don't want to learn."

"Don't be chicken," he said. "You have to keep the boat into the wind while I put the sails up."

"What if I do something wrong?" she said nervously, stepping behind the wheel to clutch it with sweating palms. Chad stood behind her with his arms around her waist.

"Turn it to port a little," he said. "We want to be heading for that promontory over there."

"To the left?" she asked, and when he affirmed that, she spun the wheel. The boat made a sudden, wide, surging curve.

"Just a *little*!" said Chad. "Bring her back around."

"Maybe you'd better do it," she said nervously.

He moved his hands down over her hips. "Nonsense. You're doing beautifully." A slight pause, and further exploration. "What did you do with your panties, dear?" He lowered his head to her neck and nuzzled behind her ear. He wore no shirt, and his bare chest was hot against her thin dress.

"Cut that out!" she said. "You're going to make me run into something."

Chad raised his head and scanned around the boat. "There is nothing to run into." He kissed her again.

The heat began to curl through her, just the way it always did whenever he touched her. She took a deep, trembling breath. "I am about to forget that I am supposed to be learning to love you."

"It's all right to forget it for a little while," he told her.

He had to stop this! Three more minutes and they would be thrashing in passion on the exposed deck of a boat in the open ocean. "Chad! Put the sails up and make some coffee!"

"All right, Hard-hearted Hannah," he said, giving her a pat on the rear. "Have it your way. Turn this scow into the wind."

"How do I do that?"

He pointed up. "See that little ribbon up there on the mast? Watch which way it blows when I get the engine stopped, then turn the boat so that it's streaming directly behind us."

She did. "I can't keep it exactly right." The little dingy, which they had towed along behind them, swung against the bigger boat like a puppy nuzzling up to its mother.

"That's good enough." He pulled on a rope and the jib unfurled. Then he raised the mainsail and came back to take the helm. The boat heeled and surged forward.

Dyana gasped, and Chad grinned at her. "The boat's supposed to tilt," he said. "And you could walk faster than we're moving."

"If you fall off, could you swim faster than we're moving? I don't want to be alone out here," Dyana said.

"I couldn't fall off in this wind. I'd have to be pushed, and since you're such a nervous nellie, I don't think I have to worry about that."

"Not if you behave yourself," she said. "How do I make coffee, and what's for breakfast?"

"There isn't any coffee, and we're having stale crackers and champagne for breakfast," he said, gazing into the distance and adjusting the sails to better catch the wind. "We'll pick up some groceries at the Narrows."

God, he was gorgeous! His hair glinted bronze in the sun, several shades lighter than his dark tan. His muscles bulged as he trimmed the sails, leaning out from the wheel to tighten the ropes. Dyana sighed. No wonder every woman in California wanted him. She couldn't blame them. She just didn't know how she could possibly compete.

"When do we get there?"

"Another couple of hours. If you feel like you can't last that long, I'll anchor and see what I can do to distract you." He waggled his eyebrows at her, looking just like the wolf in a Looney Tunes cartoon of Red Riding Hood.

Dyana laughed. "You just keep right on trucking for the harbor, Bluebeard. What is St. Michael's and why are we going there?"

"It's a cute little town—all kinds of crafts shops and antiques to browse through. You'll like it. Then we'll sail up Thompson's Creek to an old plantation house I think you'd like to see, then we'll anchor out, swim, have a picnic, and spend the night."

"I can't swim," Dyana reminded him. "My mother told you that."

"I thought she was kidding. Everybody can swim."

"Everybody but me." She put a cushion behind her and propped herself against the cabin. The breeze caught her dress and blew it above her knees. Belatedly she remembered her lack of underwear and pulled the skirt down to wrap it around her legs.

"How come you never learned?" said Chad, who had been very interested in what the breeze revealed.

"Because I refused."

"Well, I'll teach you, then," he said, looking at her fondly.

She smiled up at him. She really was in grave danger. How could any man be so thoroughly appealing? Chad had always been charming. He was now, just as he had predicted, irresistible. She regretted sleeping alone the night before—such a waste of valuable time.

"I don't want to know how to swim," she said, closing her eyes against the sight of him. "But if I were going to let anyone teach me, it would be you."

"You have to learn to swim, baby."

"Why?" she said. The sun was shining fully on the deck and the warmth was making her lazy.

"Because after we're married, I want to buy a boat like this. Besides, how will it look to our children if their mother can't swim?"

"I'm not going to marry you, so there is no point in my learning to swim." She kept her eyes lowered so he couldn't see her expression, but her tone was beginning to sound patent and not at all sincere.

Chad grinned at her. "We'll discuss it when you're in the water."

"I don't have a bathing suit."

He leered. "Good. I don't have one, either. Where are you going?"

"To dress."

"Come back here. You're dressed well enough for me."

"I'll bet," said Dyana. "You lecher, you."

"What a terrible waste of natural talent," Chad said lamentably. "You move so well underneath that dress. I believe that is the most revealing dress I ever saw. Don't ever wear it in public again."

"Ha ha," said Dyana, and disappeared below. When she came topside again, she had put on a big shirt, which she tied over the top of the dress, a pair of sandals, and a full complement of underwear.

Chad looked at her regretfully. "I'll try to remember

what you look like underneath all those clothes," he said, "until it's time for our swimming lesson. Meanwhile I have a little job for you to do."

"What?" Perhaps doing something else would take her mind off him. God knows she needed the distraction, she thought with a frustrated sigh.

"See that book of nautical charts there, on the seat? Find the one that shows the enlargement of the Kent Island Narrows."

"Okay. I've got it." She showed it to him.

He pointed at a long, narrow channel, printed in white, and told her how to read the channel markers.

"What happens if we miss one?" she wanted to know.

"The bay's only two feet deep outside this channel. If we run aground and have to call the Coast Guard to rescue us, it's damned embarrassing."

"When do I have to start looking for the markers?"

"In a while. I'll let you know." He stood easily, with one wrist draped over the wheel. His eyes were narrowed to counteract the glare off the water, and he swept his glance back and forth, scanning for markers, boats, or other obstructions.

Dyana, after a fond glance at him, put the cushion behind her head and covered her face with the chart book. "All this motion makes me sleepy," she said.

"Not queasy, are you?" Chad wondered.

"Not me," she said. "Don't worry. All I want is a nap. This is like being rocked in a cradle." Images of Chad, half clothed, spun in her head. As she lay there her thoughts became fragmented and began to make no sense. *I believe I am going to sleep*, she thought, surprised, and the images faded away altogether.

Some time later she felt Chad shaking the toe of her sneaker.

"Hey, Sleeping Beauty," he said. "The channel is just ahead."

She sat up, alarmed and fully awake. "What do I do? How fast do I have to do it?"

"We are going just about two miles an hour. We are not in any hurry." He turned the boat into the wind, furled the jib, and released the main. "Go below and pour two glasses of champagne. Drink one of them before you come back up here, then fill it again and bring one to me."

"Two glasses of champagne on an empty stomach at ten in the morning will make me drunk."

"It will make you less nervous. You are too tense to get drunk. Go on." He made shooing motions with his hand.

Well, maybe a little champagne might do her some good. She wasn't exactly relaxed. While she was pouring it she heard footsteps on the deck above her. She stuck her head out of the hatch to find that Chad was tying the mainsail neatly around the boom, and . . . my god! there was nobody driving the boat!

"Get back down there!". she yelled, horrified. "You're not even watching where we're going. We'll run into something."

"How can we run into something if we're not moving?" Chad asked, mumbling around the ties in his mouth.

"Don't try to be reasonable," said Dyana irritably, looking around her to find that they were indeed dead in the water. "It is very annoying for you to be reasonable when I want to panic."

"I know." He finished with the ties and set the glasses of champagne on the deck. "I remember."

"You do?" she asked.

When she climbed out of the cabin, he took her hands and pulled her into his embrace. "I sure do," he said. "Remember when you let Phillip think Darcy was a prostitute, and then you wanted me to call the vice squad?"

"Your plan was better, I suppose? We nearly killed him when we slugged him with that gin bottle."

"We?"

"Me, then. But," she said accusingly, "you were supposed to tackle him. The gin bottle was just a backup in case he didn't go down."

"I never had a chance to tackle him, slugger." He rubbed his nose across hers, and she slipped her arms around his neck, more than willing to be kissed. "You were too fast for me."

The skipper and crew of a passing boat whistled and cheered.

She pulled away from him and looked around. More boats were coming up behind them. "I'm not too fast for you now," she commented.

"Not yet, you're not," he agreed. "But drink the rest of that champagne and we'll see if I can keep up with you then." He started the engine and headed into the channel.

"Why can't we keep the sails up?"

"We can, but this gives us more maneuverability. It really is narrow water here." He pointed directly in front of the boat. "See down yonder? The markers are tall poles with signs on the tops. We want to keep the red signs on our left and the green signs on our right."

She searched nervously, checking the charts against what she found. One by one they passed the channel markers until they rounded a spit of land into the Narrows proper. A deep harbor had been dredged out, and an anchorage built. A raised drawbridge stretched from shore to shore across the narrow channel.

"Hot dog!" said Chad. "What timing!" He steered the

boat past the bridge just as the closing warning sounded.
Ahead was a marina with a gas dock.

"Go forward and get that rope I have curled on the
bow," he said. "When we get to the dock, a guy will
come out to help, and you just toss him the rope."

"What if it doesn't reach?"

"Fish it out of the water and throw it again," he said.
Then he added encouragingly, "Look how well you did
with the channel markers."

But it did reach, and as soon as the boat was tied,
Chad led Dyana into a ship chandler's store, which had
everything from sail maker's needles to plastic wineglasses to a grocery section full of enticing things to eat.

When they reboarded the boat, they had sacks of
crushed ice, more wine, four kinds of cheese, two
loaves of French bread, a tin of pâté, a roll of summer
sausage, a set of the wineglasses, mustard, hot dogs,
potato chips, marshmallows, matches, a package of
chocolate creme cookies, and a gallon of orange juice.

"That ought to hold us until tomorrow," said Chad
with satisfaction as he unloaded the spoils into the bulkhead storage.

"It ought to hold us till next week," said Dyana. She
took a handful of cookies and watched while Chad cast
off for St. Michael's.

The blue sky was beginning to fill with small cu-
mulus clouds, a result of the heat and humidity rising
off the bay. There was just enough breeze to move the
boat but not enough to ruffle the water. The sail to St.
Michael's was reassuring. Dyana quit thinking about
falling overboard or sinking the boat. She might, she
thought as the little town came into view, even learn to
enjoy this sort of thing, if she did enough of it. By the
time they had tied up at the dock, she was eager to get
off the *Pretty Baby* and do some exploring. Chad's

promise of antiques was alluring. She had visions of filling a house with them someday.

Chad was surprisingly interested, asking questions as they shopped, stopping to examine pieces that caught his eye and wanting to know how to tell whether they were authentic. One shop had a wonderful painted Pennsylvania Dutch hutch over one hundred and fifty years old.

"That would look absolutely wonderful in one of those big old kitchens that have fireplaces in them," said Dyana. "And a random plank floor. And big doors that open onto a lawn."

Chad ran his fingers over the wood and examined the faded blue paint critically. "It needs repainting."

The owner of the store gasped with horror, and Dyana laughed. "You destroy its value if you repaint it," she explained.

"You mean the worse it looks, the better it is?" he asked.

"Well, not exactly. Besides, don't you think this is pretty? Look at the hearts and doves painted on it."

He cocked his head and looked at it for a minute. "I guess it *is* kind of nice."

"Can't you see it in a kitchen, full of cups and plates and children's toys?"

He turned to the proprietor. "How much does it cost?"

He didn't bat an eyelash when she said six thousand dollars. "Okay. I'll buy it," he told her. "Can you hold it till I arrange for it to be shipped?"

"Chad!" said Dyana. "What in the world are you going to do with that? You live in an apartment in Los Angeles."

"I have a spot in mind for it" was all he would say. "Are you ready to go back to the boat? I want to spend the afternoon picnicking."

This time Chad took the boat a short distance and turned into what looked like a wide inlet but which, upon further travel, turned out to be the mouth of a river. It was a beautiful little river, clean and clear, and had just one small town along its banks. For the next hour they passed only trees overhanging the water, the nests of water birds, and an occasional sandy bank. There were no boats at all. Finally Chad dropped the sails, started the engine, and pulled in as close to the shore as the shallow water would permit.

"Here we are," he said.

Dyana looked up a large sloping field to a brick house about a quarter of a mile away. It wasn't terribly large, as she had imagined a plantation house to be, but was gracefully designed, with a large brick veranda facing the river and a stone path that led to a rotting pier that jutted out into the water. It looked a little seedy with age but essentially sturdy, and though some of its windows were cracked and the shutters on the brick walls needed paint, it had a homey, comfortable feeling about it. She could imagine the generations of children that had run across the wide lawns, the noise that had filled it, the happiness its families had known there.

"Why in the world is a place like this vacant, Chad?" she asked. "It's too wonderful for words."

"It is, isn't it? Come on. Let's take the dinghy up and look it over."

"Are you sure it's all right? Who owns the place?"

He gave her an extremely smug, self-satisfied look. "I do," he said. "That hutch is for the kitchen. *Now* will you marry me?"

CHAPTER
Nine

THEY TOOK A PICNIC to the shore and laid out a blanket in the cool shade under one of the big trees behind the house. It was very warm in the sun. Chad wore only a brief pair of shorts, and Dyana was glad she'd put on the loose knit dress, which was cooler even than shorts and a T-shirt would have been.

The neglected field of tall grass had once been a tidy lawn. Beginning at the old pier and curving to follow the woods at the side was a stone path that looked as if it had been laid at the same time the house was built. Here and there beside the stones were clumps of flowers or flowering bushes, laid in designs that Dyana could imagine had been carefully and lovingly planned, but the huge expanse of lawn was left uncluttered, as if for playing fields or horses.

At the point where the line of trees passed the house, the direction of the path changed, leading to the edge of the veranda. Two big oaks shaded the veranda from the afternoon sun, and along one side of the house a scraggy boxwood grew, the tiny-leaved version that Colonial gardeners had used for mazes and decorative borders.

The closer they got to the house, the more appealing it became. Its red bricks were dulled and softened by the years. Here and there patches of ivy climbed the walls and circled around the windows, draping over the shutters as neatly as if they'd been arranged by a loving hand. Wide French doors opened from the veranda to the house, and Chad fitted an old-fashioned iron key to the lock and threw open the large room inside to the fresh summer air.

Inside, Chad and Dyana wandered hand in hand through the big rooms, whose huge windows flooded them with August light. Up the wide curving stairs was a landing, where it looked as if generations of brides had made grand entrances, and the fireplaces in each of the six bedrooms were decorated with Dutch tiles, each set in a different color and telling a different story.

"I always thought this one looked like a kid's room," said Chad, opening the door to a bright corner room with a yellow-tiled fireplace.

Dyana leaned out one of the windows and looked at the ground. "I used to climb out of my windows and jump to the ground when I was about four," she said.

Chad thought of her house. "It must be fifteen feet to the ground. Why'd you do it?"

"Didn't want to take naps."

He leaned on the sill beside her. "We'll have to put bars on these windows," he said, as if he could already see small black-haired sprites determined to escape their beds.

Dyana wandered into the hall again, opening doors. "The bathrooms are pretty primitive," she said, "although I'm pretty crazy about these claw-foot tubs."

"If you think the bathrooms are bad, wait until you see the kitchen," Chad warned her. He led her downstairs, along a hall, and stood back so she could see.

"Oh, ugh!" she said, and he laughed.

The kitchen had been modernized with the latest appliances around 1927. An ugly old porcelain gas stove squatted like a trespasser inside a wonderful, huge fireplace, and half a mile or so from that was what Dyana supposed to be a refrigerator. It was about four feet tall, its cooling coils perched on top of it like a metal bird's nest. Freestanding metal cabinets had been brought in to line the walls, interrupted once to make room for some bare pipes and a concrete sink. The cabinets covered the lower windows and blocked out half the light.

"What kind of a vandal could do something like this?" she wanted to know.

"Obviously decorated before the Environmental Protection Act," said Chad. "Clear all this awful stuff out of here and it'll look real pretty. The hutch can go here by the door."

It amused her to find that a man as blatantly male as Chad could have such homey concerns.

"Maybe you should go into home decorating during the off-season," she said teasingly, preceding him out the kitchen door.

Just beside the wide brick step grew the remnants of what once must have been a little kitchen garden. Blooming around the edges, between the basil and thyme gone wild, were purple-and-yellow pansies. Chad bent and picked a few blossoms, then tucked them among the soft dark curls around Dyana's face. Finally, when her head was wreathed in them like a crown, he kissed the shining hair.

"You are so beautiful," he said softly.

Though he held her gently, loosely, she could feel the strength in his arms, the hard-muscled length of his body heated her own, and the heat was like fire from the center of the sun.

Then suddenly it was as if he could contain himself no longer. All the rigid self-control he had exercised for the past few days deserted him. He crushed her against him almost savagely, and her passion was so great that she surrendered to him with abandon. She had not suspected, she thought with fleeting amazement, that she could need him like this, with such a raging, consuming physical need. Even that night at his apartment, when they had so unexpectedly come together, her need had not been as strong as this.

Her face turned up to his, her mouth parted, hungry for his kiss, and he groaned deep in his throat as his lips met hers. The feel of him, hot and hard against her, aroused her beyond bearing.

"Please," she murmured when she could speak, and then his mouth took her again. His arms lifted her and carried her to the soft blanket under the concealing tree.

Chad set her gently on her feet and ran his hands under the soft dress to raise it over her head. She loosened his shorts and let them fall to the ground. She had never realized how beautiful he was—not a god but a flesh-and-blood man, as perfect as Adam in this Eden he had intended just for her. He was perfect—and perfectly human. His lean body was sculpted by the hours of physical activity into a form more perfect than any Michelangelo had ever made, more beautiful than any artist could create. Every muscle was cleanly outlined beneath the bronzed skin. The triangle of golden hair on his chest, lightened by hours in the sun, circled around the flat, brown nipples, which were beaded with passion now like hers and pointed like an arrowhead to his hard-muscled abdomen—and below. She laid her hands on his hips, not quite daring yet to touch him the way she wanted to.

He moved across her face with his fingers, brushing lightly across her eyelids, smoothing at her high cheekbones, outlining her swollen lips. What he touched, he kissed—the frantic pulse in her throat; her taut breasts, freed from the confining bra; her belly; and as he swiftly removed the lacy panties he put his lips to the soft skin he exposed. His tongue caressed her gently, and his fingers stroked and probed and set her on fire. It was wonderful, wonderful, this gift he gave. How selfish of her, she thought, never to give in return. So she knelt before him and took him in her hands.

"Ah, God, Dyana!" he gasped. She had no doubt that she was giving him the kind of joy she had received, and she marveled at the feel of him, so smooth and taut, so perfectly made to give her pleasure, as she was made to pleasure him.

In a moment she lay back, and he covered her with his body. She was ready for him, so ready, and he filled her completely—her body, her soul, her heart, her mind. The answer to the question in her heart was answered—she loved him. Had loved him always, would never stop loving him.

He lay kissing her, and she moved against him impatiently.

"Don't you want to make this last a little longer?" he asked teasingly, and moved slightly, just enough to tantalize.

"Chad," she moaned. "Don't torture me."

"I can if I torture myself, too," he said, and he began to move slowly inside her, long, slow strokes that teased but didn't satisfy. She grasped him tightly and arched against him, mutely begging for more. He chuckled and continued, just a little faster, a little deeper.

"Chad!" she begged. "Please!"

Finally he could stand it no longer himself, and did exactly what she wanted him to do. The heat of the day and the heat of their passion merged and exploded together—unforgettable pleasure, in an unforgettable place, on a day she would remember forever as the day she opened her life at last to the liberating possibilities of love.

Dyana didn't get back to Chicago until late Sunday night. She and Chad had parted at the Baltimore airport after a furtive evening avoiding public places. Susan met her plane at midnight.

"You must have had quite a time" were her first words.

"Why?" asked Dyana.

Susan looked at her curiously. "You mean, you don't know?"

"Know what?" asked Dyana with a feeling of dread.

"Never mind," said Susan. "It can wait."

"What can wait?"

"I don't want to talk about it here."

Whatever it was, it must have been horrible. There was nothing in the world Susan loved better than a good, juicy, shocking tale. And when she was suddenly so circumspect, it created all sorts of suspicion in Dyana's mind.

When they got to Dyana's apartment, Susan got out of the car and locked it. "Mind if I come in for a glass of wine?" she asked.

"It's midnight," Dyana protested, then she realized that Susan had been chattering about inconsequential things all the way home. "Got something to tell me?"

"Yeah, and you're probably not going to like it."

Dyana stopped at her mailbox and picked up her newspaper. When they got into her living room, Susan said, "I'll pour the wine. You look at the paper."

"Just tell me what it is you want me to know," said Dyana. "I don't want to read the paper."

"Yes you do," Susan told her, and she disappeared into the kitchen.

When Susan left the room, Dyana got on her hands and knees and called Josie. The little gray cat stuck her head out from under the couch and looked around for strangers (everybody but Dyana was a stranger as far as Josie was concerned), then jumped into Dyana's arms and purred. Dyana settled on the couch with Josie on her lap and unfolded the newspaper.

At the top, above the headline, it read, WEBER PICKS A HOMETOWN HONEY.

She turned the pages frantically, searching for the article. But when she found it, she discovered that it wasn't just an article. It was an article and a picture.

The picture the photographer on the street had taken through their hotel window. Worse, it was a wire release. That meant it was probably in every paper in the nation.

And it wasn't even in the news. It was in the People and Places section, which was just a fancy name for the gossip column. Usually the columnist effervesced over the city's powerful politicians or the Chicago upper crust. But today practically every inch was taken by Chad Weber and Dyana Kincaid. She saw their names in boldface type, but she couldn't bring herself to read the article yet. Besides, the picture was arresting.

If she'd been judging the picture on its artistic merits, she'd have given it a prize. She and Chad were clearly outlined against the light behind them. Their features were just barely visible, just enough to show the passion on their faces. Their eyes were closed, their heads tilted, their lips parted and about to meet. Her arms pulled him close, and one of her hands pushed through his thick hair, and it was caught in her fingers as if she never intended to let him go. His hands—she hadn't remembered when this had happened!—were cupped around her bottom, lifting her into him. All in all, it was a picture that would make anybody's heart beat faster, a picture that might be banned in Boston, fuel gossip from coast to coast, and cause at least four heart attacks, one of which was not the one Dyana thought she was having now.

"Oh, my God!" she breathed. "This is horrible!"

"Isn't it?" said Susan cheerfully, handing her a full glass of Italian red wine. "What are you going to do about it?"

Josie, alarmed at Susan's presence, dug her claws into Dyana's leg and yowled. Dyana heartlessly shooed her away and sank back against the soft cushions. "I am going to have to quit my job. If they don't fire me. I think there's a morals clause in my contract."

"Don't be silly," Susan said scoffingly. "You'll rise to heights of prestige you never even dreamed of. Every man in the world will look at you through new eyes. If you don't want Chad, you can have anybody."

"Please, Susan!" Dyana groaned. "I need sympathy, not jokes."

"Who's kidding whom? I'd go for money if I were you," she advised. "Money lasts. Looks don't. I mean, like my mother always says, its just as easy to love a rich man as a poor one."

Dyana drained her wineglass. "I hate to think what *my* mother is going to say." She looked at the picture again and steeled herself to read the caption below.

"She's going to say, 'Grab him before he gets away,'" Susan told her.

"She's going to say, 'what am I supposed to tell your grandmother?'"

"Your grandmother will be thrilled. She's wanted you to get married for five years. And look at all the new opportunities. Just remember I'm your best friend," said Susan. "And pass the better rejects on to me. I'm not desperate yet, but every woman needs to improve her chances."

"Susan!" Dyana protested. "There aren't going to be any 'new opportunities.'"

"Nonsense," said Susan briskly. "Be an optimist. Now, remember that I like sort of short ones—they make better lovers than the tall guys because they try so hard to compensate for not having long legs."

Dyana smiled. "Not necessarily," she said, remembering the afternoon she'd spent on the blanket behind the big house.

Susan saw the look on her face. "So what happened while you were away with the world's sexiest man?"

"Take a look. We were followed by photographers, reporters, and autograph seekers until we were nearly driven mad."

"Is that *all*?" Susan asked, disappointed. "I want to hear the rest of it."

Dyana was reading the story underneath the picture. It gave a pretty clear picture of Chad Weber. When he wasn't being an offensive end, he was busy knocking down—or up—every woman under fifty in Southern California. Every woman his name had been linked with in the past five years was listed in the column, together with quotes from several who intimated that they were willing to 'tell all' if the price was right. The picture they painted of Dyana was pretty clear, too. It made her sound like a woman on the make, somebody who was just after Chad for his body.

Well, quipped an imp in her mind, what exactly had she been after the previous day when they were lying on that blanket? His wit? His charm? His money? His fame?

The columnist said she had it on good authority that there was a betting pool going on in the Crusaders' locker room as to just how long this romance would last. After all, she finished gaily, Chicago was a long way from Los Angeles, and there were plenty of women

just waiting for a chance to show the fabulous Mr.
Weber that he didn't need to be lonesome—because, of
course, Chad had always been a man who took his fun
where he could find it.

Dyana had never realized that she could actually
snarl. She stalked from the couch to the bedroom and
spent a sleepless night, alternating between rage and de-
spair. The trouble was, she loved Chad. She just
couldn't believe he loved her. If he loved her, why
hadn't he called? If he didn't love her, why would he
treat her this way? After all, he had loved her once, and
she refused to believe that the honorable boy she had
known had turned into a deceitful, dishonorable man.
He wouldn't just use her, he'd tell her lies *and* use her.
If she was sure of anything, she was sure of that. And
on that note she rolled over and closed her eyes and
tried to sleep.

Her alarm rang at six. Josie jumped onto the bed,
meowing. She only did that when her food dish was
empty. The food dish was only empty when Dyana was
completely out of cat food. She petted Josie disconso-
lately.

"I'll tell you what, Josie," she said. "You go to
school for me today and I'll go to the store and get you
a fresh fish and chopped liver." Josie crawled under the
bed and stayed there.

Darcy called at five after six.

"Oh, Darcy," Dyana wailed, "what in the world am I
going to do? I can't show my face in school."

"Seems to me I've heard you say that before," said
Darcy. "Maybe ten thousand times. You shouldn't be so
impulsive," she added, unable to resist teasing her.

"Everybody in the whole United States has seen that
picture," said Dyana.

"Not everybody," said Darcy. "I hid it from my children. I won't show it to them till they grow up and are able to understand."

"That's very funny," said Dyana. "I'm dying laughing."

"Seriously, Dyana, it's not as bad as you think it is," Darcy said soothingly. "Just a picture of a man and a woman kissing."

"Taken through a hotel window with a telephoto lens, which is pointed out in the caption. It leaves *everything* to the imagination. Nobody knows what happened after that."

"What did happen?" asked Darcy curiously.

"Absolutely nothing! We went to dinner!"

Darcy's chuckle came through the line. "I can well imagine you might have trouble getting anyone but me to believe that story. And I'm having a little trouble."

"I can't talk about this anymore," said Dyana. "I want to get to school before the janitor does. I am going to sit in my office all day with the door shut."

"Call me," instructed Darcy, "just as soon as you walk through the door tonight. I want to know about the weekend, and I don't want to hear it all secondhand, from Susan."

Josie twined between her ankles as she searched through her closet for something suitably unbecoming to wear. If she looked awful enough, nobody could possibly think that she and Chad had done exactly what they did. She sure hadn't looked awful in that picture. Damn knit dress. She was going to cut it up and make rags of it. If she'd had on a sensible skirt and blouse, or even jeans, the picture wouldn't have looked nearly as compromising as it had.

Oh, rats. In a long, horrible career of getting into trouble at school, this was the worst trouble yet. Everybody was going to smirk at her all day. And the students! What in the world was she going to tell all the students who wanted help managing their love lives? Under the circumstances, "Just say no" might seem a little hypocritical.

The trouble with the summer-school session, she thought, pulling into the parking lot, was that the sun came up so early. There were already people in the building, and they looked at her curiously when they greeted her. She had found a shapeless blue cotton sweater in one of her drawers and had put it on over a dark paisley cotton skirt, and she pulled the sweater down nervously each time she passed someone on the way to her office. As a consequence, by the time she had made the journey, the poor sweater was stretched completely over her hips.

The department secretary looked up as Dyana came in. "Have a nice weekend?" she asked, and then she grinned.

"Oh, God, Mildred," said Dyana. "Not you, too."

"Yep," said Mildred. "Me, too. Have a good day!"

Mildred was the first but not the last. The football coach called. Did Dyana think she could get Chad to come talk to the boys?

The school principal called. Did Dyana think perhaps Chad might be one of the speakers at graduation?

The superintendent of schools called. Would Dyana mind getting an autograph for his eight-year-old grandson?

So much for public scandal.

The students asked what the adults were afraid to ask. One after another, as if they were all on tape, they said, "Are you going to marry him, Miss Kincaid?"

She really didn't know what to say. She couldn't say he hadn't asked her yet, because he had. She couldn't say she hadn't made up her mind, because she tried that, and the interrogator wanted to know if Chad had popped the question.

Finally, unable to stand it anymore, she wrote out a statement in black marker and posted it on the bulletin board outside the office: "Dyana Kincaid will let you know who she plans to marry when she finds the right man. The information will be posted on this spot. Keep breathing while you wait for further developments."

It worked for most of the day, but as she was getting ready to sneak out of her office for the safety of her car, one bold imp with red hair and braces wanted to know if she and Chad loved each other.

That one was hard to answer. She was pretty sure about herself. She was even pretty sure about Chad, when she was alone with him. The trouble was, they had been alone together exactly two days in the last ten years. She didn't see how a young love like that could have kept its fire all those years, although she didn't question that when she was in Chad's arms. She had thought about him every single second since he had kissed her good-bye in the airport in Baltimore—but had he thought about her? He hadn't called. She had expected him to get in touch with her by now and she was feeling insecure, and though she wouldn't have admitted it for the world, her feelings were hurt.

Besides, what was love? She didn't really know Chad anymore. She had known and loved the boy. Did she love the man, or was she just reacting to a wonderful memory and his enormous sexuality? Perhaps her emotions were fooling her, and two days was simply not enough time to decide, particularly as Chad was so forceful and so persuasive that it was almost impossible to tell whether she loved him because she loved him, or whether she loved him because he commanded her to.

She had to force herself to concentrate on her driving. Whenever she dropped her guard, her thoughts drifted to Chad. His face. His eyes, dark with passion after he kissed her; the way his lips looked just before

they met hers. His voice telling her he loved her. His
touch proving it in a thousand wonderful ways. His
fingers feather-light across her breasts; his hands gentle
on her hips.

A billboard advertising a pet store flashed past. Cat-
food, Dyana thought, and wheeled into the next super-
market.

She intended to get only cat food, so she didn't get a
basket. And she needed milk, she remembered, and
chicken cutlets were on sale. And tomato juice; she
liked it for breakfast. She picked up the largest can they
had. And paper towels—she was completely out of
paper towels. And eggs. But it didn't matter how she
juggled the items in her arms, she couldn't handle the
eggs without dropping them. Thus loaded, she stood in
a checkout line that had seven people ahead of her, all
with full baskets. The express line wasn't open.

Gradually she became aware that there was somebody looking at her, examining her so closely that it
made the hair on the back of her neck prickle. There
was a man behind her, and when she turned around, he
smiled.

"Aren't you the girl in the picture this morning?" he
asked. He didn't need to say what picture; the leer in his
eye told her.

"No," she said, and faced the counter again.

He moved in even closer. "Yes you are," he said in
what he obviously thought was a seductive tone. "You
know, I went to school with Weber. He isn't so much. I
could give you more than that."

"Get away from me," said Dyana. Oh, God. She'd
looked like a whore in that picture. She knew it. And
here was the slimy living proof, behind her. "Get away
from me or I'll scream."

"You could be a little friendly, honey," the man said.

"You were certainly friendly enough with him."

Dyana wasn't scared anymore. She was furious. She looked down. He was wearing sneakers. She carefully set her other items down, then threw the heavy can of tomato juice at his foot. When she was certain that he was disabled, she put five dollars on the counter for the cat food and left the store.

But she was trembling so, she could hardly drive, and her hands were still shaking when she tried to put the key in the lock. She collapsed into one of her kitchen chairs, nearly in tears, and sat there while Josie purred around her ankles. She picked the little cat up and buried her hot face in Josie's soft fur.

Chad still hadn't called. And what was she going to tell him when he did? That she wasn't safe on the streets, thanks to their weekend in Baltimore? That an entire nation of men considered her fair game?

She sat at her kitchen table and watched Josie eat. When the phone rang, she no longer expected it to be Chad. When she heard his voice, her heart leapt with joy.

"Hi, darling," he said. "Set the date for our wedding yet?"

"Hi, yourself," she said, giddy with relief. "I'm not setting the date till I find out why you haven't called me."

"I've been running plays since six-thirty this morning. I just got home." He did sound tired. "I was going to take a nap so I could stay awake long enough to tell you how much I love you, but I thought I'd better call early so I could warn you. You hate this sort of thing so much, I wouldn't want you to find out from everybody else."

Irrationally with a feeling of panic, she thought, *He doesn't want me, after all. All this was just a sham.* She clutched at the little crystal around her neck; solid proof of his love, a talisman.

Chad continued, sounding half amused and half apologetic. She could almost see the lopsided smile and the blue, blue eyes that could melt her heart.

"We're the feature attraction on the evening news."

CHAPTER
Ten

DYANA WAS SUDDENLY queasy. She went into the living room and turned on the TV.

The picture bobbled a little as the camera man was jostled, but the images were all too clear. Dyana stared at the picture on the screen. She stood slightly behind Chad, who looked angry, and the light of the camera, hitting the dock house on the pier in Baltimore Harbor, put her partly in the shade and distorted her shape. Her normally rounded, very feminine figure looked voluptuous. Her hair was tousled, and her lips looked a little swollen and very well kissed. She looked wanton and much younger than she was, the kind of woman men used for pleasure and discarded easily.

"Chad Weber," said the commentator, "connoisseur of fast women, fast cars, fast horses, and fast living, has surprised a bevy of California beauties by taking up a hometown girl as his Woman of the Week. Dyana Kincaid was his kindergarten pal and his high-school sweetheart, so perhaps the fickle Charming Chad will see his young man's fancy turn to love and let the luscious, long-legged, raven-locked Miss Kincaid linger, at least for a while."

The phone rang.

"Oh, no," Dyana said out loud. "Not already."

But it was Chad. "Pretty good picture, huh? Better than the one in the paper."

She exploded. "Pretty good picture! Do you know what I've been through all day, just because of that picture in the paper?"

"Yeah," said Chad. "I've come in for a little teasing, myself. One of the guys put a dime-store frame on it and hung it in my locker."

"You enjoy this, don't you?" she said, enraged by his attitude. She'd been through hell all day. The least he could do was appreciate it.

"Sure," he admitted. "Most of it. Hell, the fans mean well, Dyana, most of them. They just like a little reflected glory. Makes them feel important. And you're a beautiful woman—the guy on the TV was right about that, Miss Luscious, Long-legged, Raven-haired Kincaid. You're not some dumpy little pudding-faced nobody. Why *wouldn't* they fight to get pictures of you?"

"Was he right about you and the Woman of the Week, Charming Chad?" There was acid in her tone, concealing the fear underneath.

"I told you those women were mostly for show. I haven't had any serious relationships, except for one, since I left you. And I never will again."

"What about the unserious, just-for-fun little flings?"

Chad's voice was cold. "I have better things to do than fight over two thousand miles of copper wire."

"I'm not trying to fight!" Dyana said. "I'm trying to find out what kind of man you are."

"I'd think you'd already know that," he said. "Think about it. And while you're thinking about it, try to remember that I love you. What I said to you, what I did, wasn't just some ploy to get you into bed with me. I don't have to go to that much trouble if I just want a warm body."

"What a wonderful attitude. Exactly matches your reputation as the Playboy of the Western World."

"You really want to believe I'm going to play around on you, don't you? Why? Do you plan to have a little fling or two yourself?"

"I don't think you know what you're going to do, Chad. You come home and in two days decide it's me, only me, and you'll never want another woman again. You can't decide something like that overnight. It isn't possible."

"I didn't decide overnight, Dyana. I decided when I was seventeen. Time has only made me more positive. I came to that reunion for one reason. To see you. And I expected it to hurt."

"Hurt? Why would it hurt?"

"Why wouldn't it hurt, to see you happily married? To know you were satisfied in the arms of another man? To find out you hadn't given me a thought in all that time?" He paused. "I want you to be happy, Dyana. More than anything. But I want you happy with me. Not with somebody else."

"Oh, Chad." Now was the time. She couldn't go on, forever afraid to speak. "I can't be happy with anyone else. I never have been. I'm just terribly worried, that's all. You live one kind of life, I live another. I don't know if I can adjust to it."

"You can try, can't you?" He was not really asking. His tone of voice said he expected her to do it, and not make too much of a fuss.

Aren't you willing to make any adjustments for me? Can't you help me some? she asked silently. Aloud she said, "Yes."

As if in answer to her unspoken question, he said,

"We'll see what we can do to minimize the impact of all this publicity. It's a little hard to get used to, I expect."

"Did you find it hard to get used to?"

"It sort of grew as I did. A little of it in high school, more of it in college, more and more as I got better at my job. So it came on gradually, not all at once. The trick is not to believe all the hype."

"How can you help it?" she said, remembering some of the flattering things she'd heard about Chad over the years.

"Because if you start believing what they say about you in the news media, you're ruined. If it's good, you get to thinking the world can't get along without you, which sets you up for an awful fall when the hard times come. And if it's bad, you start believing you're completely no good and don't amount to anything, so you quit trying. Either way, it'll kill you."

Dyana began to have a glimmering idea that perhaps Chad's life wasn't as easy as she thought it was. "Believe nothing of what you hear and half of what you see?"

"Don't believe anything of either one." He gave a sort of half laugh. "The job of the media is to manufacture news. When there isn't any, they make some up. Remember that."

"I'll try."

"Just do what I do—try to have fun with it. The autographs and the people wanting to pat my shoulder. Like that. And it is fun, Dyana. You'll see."

"I will?" she said. She certainly hadn't had fun with it yet. She couldn't imagine that being portrayed as the Woman of the Week could ever be any fun.

"You will," he said positively. "Hey, are you still wearing our crystal?"

She touched it and smiled. "I am." She could still

feel this touch at her throat, warm and sensual, and she longed for him to come home.

"When do you want to get married?"

"Chad, give me time to get used to this."

"How much time do you need? You've known me for twenty-three years. Don't you think that's a little long for an engagement?"

"The engagement has been three days."

He gave a theatrical, tragic sigh. "How soon you forget. I asked you to marry me when we were six."

"Not exactly. You said you wanted to trade the cookies in your lunch for my chocolate pudding, and when I refused, you said you'd marry me when we grew up if I'd let you have the pudding."

"That's not the way I remember it. I remember begging you to marry me, and you said you would if I'd let you have the cookies."

"Also, in second grade, when you wanted me to draw a map, you wanted me to marry you."

"I wanted you to kiss me. That was different. I was branching out a little."

She smiled at the memory. "Do you remember the first time you kissed me?"

He laughed. "How could I forget? Your braces cut my lip and it was swollen for days. All the guys thought you'd hit me."

"Worried about your reputation then, too, I gather."

"What fourteen-year-old boy isn't? I was trying to be a real suave Casanova and wound up looking like Daffy Duck."

"You have no idea how mortified I was about that kiss."

"As I recall, at the time you laughed—while you dabbed at the blood with a tissue."

"I was sure you'd never speak to me again."

"Came right back for more the next weekend. And

the weekend after that. And the one after that. I never wanted to be away from you, Dyana. I still don't."

"You could come play for the Bears," she said, teasingly.

"The weather's nicer out here, my love," he told her. "We'll buy a nice big house with a swimming pool and enough bedrooms for six kids."

"We have a house in Maryland."

"That's for off-season, sweet. Think I'd let you live that far from me?" His voice was intimate and low. "Why don't you fly out tomorrow? We'll go to Reno after the game and tie the knot."

"My mother *and* yours would have heart attacks."

"How long, then?" he said impatiently. "Dammit, Dyana, I want you *now*."

It was exhilarating to have him wanting her, loving her. She could hear it in his voice, in his impatience for their marriage, in his blithe disregard for their problems. They loved each other, reasoned Chad. Therefore they could work anything out.

Dyana almost believed it, until she looked at the picture from the newspaper. She loved him, all right. She always would, she supposed, but how was she ever going to learn to live with the lack of privacy and all the things that the media invented to titillate their audience?

For two weeks he called her every night. She watched his games on television, holding her breath every time he got tackled. Football had always seemed dangerous to her, but now it seemed positively life-threatening.

Susan laughed at her. "He's been playing football since he was in grade school. Don't you think he knows what he's doing by now? Besides, look at all the padding they wear."

"Look at all the guys they carted off the field today," Dyana retorted. "Look at all the ones who limped away to the locker rooms and couldn't finish the game. Don't try to tell me it's not dangerous."

Her mother and Chad's weren't a bit interested in the games. They were interested only in china patterns and monogrammed linens and guest lists and bridesmaids' dresses.

"You'd think they were the ones getting married," Dyana told him, laughing. "They're so excited, they can't sit still. You should see all the stuff they bring over to show me."

"How big a shindig is this going to be, anyway?" Chad asked suspiciously. "I was thinking about just maybe having my parents and yours, and Darcy and Phillip and the kids, and that's all."

"And the preacher."

"And the preacher. What are you planning, exactly?"

"Truth is, I'm not planning anything. I mentioned my family and yours and Darcy and Phillip and the kids to my mother, and I thought she was going to faint with horror." She paused for effect. "Our mothers were over here last night, with lists of things to do. This wedding isn't quite as big as the presidential inauguration, but it's moving up on it."

"Oh, God!" Chad groaned.

"Look at it from the dark side. If you don't send them a list of your friends, you won't have anybody you know there."

"How much is it going to cost?" he demanded.

"You're beginning to sound like a husband already. Looks like about ten or twelve thousand dollars."

"Oh, my God!"

"Mother says it's she and Daddy who are supposed to pay for it, but—"

"Absolutely not!" said Chad. "We're two self-sup-porting people. They're retiring in a few years. They can be just as traditional as they want to be about everything else—your father can even be archaic and give the bride away, but I will pay for my own wedding."

"I was going to say that's what I told them, before you so rudely interrupted. Do you like gold-trimmed plates or silver, or do you want flowers on them?"

"I don't care what they look like as long as they're full of food. Try to get forks that are big enough for my hand, though. I ate dinner last night with a friend of mine who just got married, and his wife had bought these little dinky forks that only had three prongs. Couldn't get anything on them. And he's a linebacker—great big huge guy. That damn fork looked like a toothpick in his hand. Silliest thing you ever saw."

"Big forks. You got it. Will a meat fork be big enough?

"I'm not sure what that is, but I think you're making fun of me."

"Just a little."

"I love you. Even if you do give me a hard time."

"I don't give you a hard time."

"Speaking of hard—"

"Don't be obscene over a public communication system."

"I miss you. I'd ask you to fly out for the weekend, but I have to work until after the Super Bowl."

"You're certainly confident."

"You bet. That's where we're headed. If a bookmaker offers good odds, take them. The Crusaders are going to the Super Bowl this year."

"How do you know?"

"Skill, knowledge of the game, the will to win, and besides, it's our turn."

"If you win the Super Bowl, you want to get married in February?"

"February!" He sounded dismayed. "I don't want to

wait until February! Let's get married now and have the honeymoon in February."

"Call my mother and ask her why that's impossible. Her schedule says that anything under a year is rushing things. I have to go. I am meeting Darcy at Marshal Field to look at china."

"Are you going to watch my game on Sunday?"

"I always watch your games, darling. I haven't missed one since you got out of college. Did you know that?"

"No." He was quiet for a second. "Try to remember, no matter what you hear, that I love you very much, Dyana."

"I'll remember," she told him, but afterward, thinking about what he'd said, she was puzzled. Was it just his distrust of the media that had prompted the request, or was there something else, something she didn't know about—something he hadn't told her?

She found out when she read the Sunday paper.

"The Crusaders' champion of fancy footwork, Chad Weber, is once again squiring around old flame Stacy Carleton. Also seen with them is Stacy's son, William. The big mystery here is, who is William's father? Stacy isn't saying, and neither is Charming Chad."

It heated Dyana's temper to the boiling point. At the very least, Chad should have told her about this instead of letting her think Stacy Carleton was in the distant, forgotten past. At the very most, Chad should have told the woman he was about to get married and to get out of town by sundown.

Dyana was in a foul mood when she reached Darcy's house, where she was supposed to watch the game. To make matters worse, the cameras took a shot of Stacy Carleton in the stands, looking much more glamorous than just plain Dyana Kincaid ever could.

It was a close game. Chad caught a long pass in the

fourth quarter and sprinted for the goal. He was just a hand's length out of the reach of the defending tackle, who was desperately trying to get within range.

"Get him," Dyana mumbled vengefully.

Darcy heard her and gave a sympathetic smile. "I read the paper, too. You don't believe that stuff about Stacy Carleton and the baby, do you?"

Dyana had the grace to look a little sheepish. "Chad keeps telling me not to believe anything I see or hear, but I tell you, Darcy, it's hard when all I hear is what a playboy he is and how he takes three different women a week to bed with him and all I see is his picture in the paper, each time with a woman who isn't me."

"He says none of that is true?"

"That's what he says." Dyana looked at the screen again. Chad, of course, had made the touchdown, and the scantily clad cheerleaders were squealing and bouncing around. Dyana had heard that some of them were happily married women. It didn't seem likely to her.

"I'd believe him if I were you," said Darcy, heading for the kitchen to get a bowl of pretzels.

"Why?" asked Dyana, tagging along after her.

"Because it's the right thing to do." Darcy turned around and took Dyana's shoulders in her hands. "Oh, look, Imp. Always believe what the man you love tells you. He's not going to lead you wrong."

Dyana sighed, trying to control her fertile imagination. "Well, maybe you're right."

That evening Chad called.

"I read the paper," said Dyana. "I am trying not to believe anything I read or anything I hear, but it's hard, because they showed a picture of Stacy Carleton sitting on the fifty-yard line looking gorgeous."

"I didn't know exactly what the papers were going to say," Chad told her. "But I knew they were going to say something. We turned up at the same party last week, and she said she didn't have a ride home, so I gave her one. A reporter saw us leave."

"Why didn't you suggest she call a taxi?" Dyana asked.

Chad laughed. "Maybe I will, next time. What did you do today, besides watch TV and wish you were here?"

She took a deep breath. "Actually I spent a lot of it wondering if her son is your son, too."

There was a long, frightening silence from Chad. Finally, when he spoke, it was obvious that he chose his words carefully.

"I know I can't make you believe me, Dyana, but I'm not his father. The fact is, Stacy slept with so many men five years ago that only she knows who that child's father is—but she's assured me that it isn't me."

"Poor little boy," said Dyana, stricken by the specter of growing up without ever having a father, or being able to find out who he really was.

"That's what I think," said Chad quietly. "I go over there because I feel so sorry for the little guy. Stacy was one of those things that happens—I was never in love with her, and I never meant anything to her. But little William needs a friend, and I try to be that friend. Stacy is all show—she totes him around with her because she likes to play the doting mother. When she's not onstage, she doesn't want to have much to do with him."

"You're sweet," she said, and meant it. Chad never could resist stray dogs or kittens or any small animal or child. Anything weak and helpless found a ready champion in him. Dyana had almost forgotten that.

"I should have told you sooner," Chad said. "He's become a permanent fixture in my life. He needs me. Do you think you can live with that?"

"I can live with anything, as long as you love me,"

she said, loving him so much that at the moment she thought her heart would burst with it.

"Can you live with me if I come home for the weekend?" he wanted to know. "We have a few days off."

He was coming home! "Don't you have to practice?"

"Yes. Four days alone with you will cost me about two thousand dollars. Five hundred a day in fines."

"That's ridiculous. Why don't I come out there?"

He met her at the airport, looking sexier than any man had a right to look. His blond hair was streaked by the sun and tousled by the wind. No wonder Stacy Carleton wanted him. Who wouldn't?

The kiss he gave her had enough power to cause a nuclear meltdown. What the kiss didn't accomplish, the feel of his hands on her back—and his long, hard length pressed against her—did. She felt as wanton as she looked at the Baltimore Harbor.

"I hope you don't want to stop anywhere on the way home," said Chad. His voice was husky with passion. "It has been a very long, very dry three weeks, and I have missed you more than I thought possible."

"I thought you'd been missing me for ten years," she said teasingly, although her own passion was dangerously near explosion. How many years could they get in jail if she threw him down on the carpeted floor of the airport corridor and tore all his clothes off?

She bet the gossip column wouldn't mention Stacy Carleton for weeks.

"Missing you and thinking I can't have you is not nearly as bad as missing you and knowing you're only a continent away." He bent her head back and kissed her again, very slowly, to the obvious delight of the passengers waiting for the next plane. "You have no idea how close I came to sticking it to the football team and coming to Chicago."

"But your enormous sense of responsibility kept you from it, right?" She smiled at him, knowing that though her tone was light, what she said was very true. Chad took his responsibilities very seriously. He always had.

She looked around her. "Hey, something's missing. Where are all the paparazzi?"

Chad grinned. "I guess they haven't tapped my phone yet. They didn't know you were coming. Won't they be disappointed when they discover they've missed a photo opportunity?" He *was* in a hurry; His long legs covered the ground rapidly. "Can't you walk any faster, honey?" He waggled his eyebrows at her. "I am in a very big hurry to get you back to the house."

Outside, instead of the red Mercedes, was an old Volkswagen beetle in jelly-bean green.

"Chad!" she said, delighted. "Where did you get this?"

"Bought it." He looked very pleased with himself. "Isn't it cute?"

"Where's the Mercedes?"

"In Chicago. I flew back, remember? Anyway, I like this better. It has real personality. I drive it all the time."

"When we get married, I want it for a wedding present. You can have the Mercedes."

"I'll buy you one of your own. I'm too selfish to give mine up."

"They don't make them anymore."

"I bought this one off a fellow who was using it as the company car for his pest-control business. It was painted gray and had mouse ears on it."

"Are you joking?"

"Would I joke about a thing like that? I had to rescue the poor little fellow. He's too old to be made fun of." Chad turned a corner into a long road that was obviously a private entrance to an exclusive residential area. Sure enough, in about a hundred yards there was a gate house. The attendant waved them through, and Chad drove around a huge lake to a stand of town houses built in the Spanish Mission style.

"These are gorgeous," she said.

"I really like mine. Wait till you see the inside."

They went through a wrought-iron gate and onto a private patio. It was tiled in turquoise and gray, and had a beautiful little fountain built into the wall. Inside, the foyer went up two stories, and the living room and dining room, both of which had a glass wall opening onto a patio with a swimming pool, were flooded with the afternoon light.

"What else is outside?" asked Dyana, going to the big glass doors.

"You can look outside later," said Chad. The smoldering expression on his face and the passionate tension in his body was enough to set her on fire.

She looked at him from under her lashes. "Aren't you going to offer me a drink?"

"It's football season. I don't drink." He was advancing toward her, step by deliberate step.

"I had an afternoon flight and didn't have time for lunch."

"Too bad," said the love of her life, who cared only for her comfort and well-being. "You'll have to go hungry for a while."

"That's not very considerate," she murmured as he reached for her.

"I'll be considerate when I get you upstairs," he promised. Then he lifted her in his arms and carried her across the wide white carpet, up the curving stairs, into the luxurious bedroom, and she never saw a bit of it, not a bit, till later. All she could see was Chad.

Four days and two thousand dollars in team fines later, Chad put Dyana on a plane for home. She still had seen very little of his town house but the bedroom, the huge whirlpool bath, and the kitchen. They hadn't watched the large-screen TV, they hadn't sat on the blue leather couch in the den, they hadn't swum in the long pool full of clear blue water. Dyana pointed this out while they waited for her flight to be called.

"We'll do it in two years," said Chad.

"Two years?"

"Yeah. I figure it will take me at least that long to make up for lost time." He laughed. "One of the guys on the team said if you put a penny in a jar every time you make love for the whole first year you're married, and then take a penny out every time you make love for the next fifty years, you never use up all the pennies. Let's try it and find out."

The flight was called for boarding. Dyana kissed him good-bye. "Be sure you buy a very big jar," she said.

She got back to Chicago and called him but only got the answering machine. She knew he was working hard —preparing for the games during the season was grueling work, she knew—but she expected to hear from him, and when she didn't, all the old fears and worries came flooding back. Between the fittings for her wedding dress and trips to find china and silverware and linens and all the other paraphernalia she needed to set up housekeeping as a married woman, she worried. And she felt too ridiculous about the worry to confide it to a soul, even Darcy.

The first game came and went. The Crusaders won. Sportswriters were already predicting a trip to the Super Bowl. Still Chad didn't call. But he was named Most Valuable Player, and the cheerleaders all crowded around him, jumping and squealing and grabbing him for kisses.

He looked like he enjoyed it, she noted with irritation.

At the beginning of the second week she got a short

note from him. "Up too early and home too late to call," it read. "I don't want to disturb your dreams of me. I'll try to call Saturday, late."

What dreams? Nightmares were what she had. Visions of cheerleaders leering, grasping, voracious, snatching him away from her. Finally she couldn't stand it anymore and told Darcy.

Darcy was very comforting and offered a lot of help. "You're crazy," she said, and that was the end of that.

Dyana was at Darcy's house to watch the Crusaders play on Friday. They won. By then the victories were becoming monotonous. Chad had made four touchdowns, floating like thistledown across the Astroturf, running so easily that it looked as if he were making no effort at all. And behind him, pursuers thundered, breathing hard, smashing to the ground as they tried desperate tackles from too far away.

After the game the cameras switched to the hall outside the locker rooms, so they could interview him. As soon as he came through the door, before they first reporter could ask a question, Stacy Carleton burst through the crowd to reach Chad. She smiled and said something that the microphone couldn't catch, and then Chad wrapped her in a binding hug and kissed her hard on the mouth. Her little boy stood beside them, and Chad picked him up. Then the three of them left the stadium with the reporters trailing after.

Phillip was the first to speak. "That SOB," he said.

"Wait a minute, there's got to be more to it than we just saw," said Darcy.

"I'm sure you're right," said Dyana bitterly. "Much more." And she gathered her coat, purse, and keys and drove herself home through a fog of unshed tears.

He had been lying to her. She believed he wanted to marry her and that he loved her. She didn't believe he intended ever to give up the other women who flocked around him. The heady sexuality of being wanted by every female in the United States was too much for him. There were many men who loved their wives but were unfaithful, not because they loved other women but because they enjoyed infidelity casually as a hobby, so to speak.

Well, she wouldn't live like that. She unearthed the Old Maid of Meadows High award and put it on the mantel. And she took the pink quartz crystal and hid it under a pile of old winter clothes in the top of her closet, where she wouldn't have to look at it every time she opened her jewelry box.

Darcy tried to reason with her, to no avail. When Chad finally called, she wouldn't talk to him. He called again, and she hung up. At last she stopped answering the phone.

The bell rang. She answered the door and there was Darcy, looking annoyed. "You know you're being stupid, don't you?"

"I am not going to talk about this."

"You have to, Imp. Do you plan to be miserable for the entire rest of your life?"

"I don't see any alternative." She turned to her sister and demanded, "Look, if that was Phillip, what would you do?"

"I'd at least listen to what he had to say. He has an explanation."

"Did Chad call you and ask you to come over here?"

Darcy looked at little embarrassed. "Well, in a word, yes. You ought to listen to the message at least."

"I don't want to. You say you'd at least listen to what Phillip had to say if I were you, but what if the same thing happened over and over again? How long would you keep listening before you decided to throw in the towel?"

Darcy didn't say anything.

"Be honest, Darcy," said Dyana. "It's important."

When Darcy spoke, it was obvious that it hurt her to say what she said. "Twice. I'd believe it once. The second time I'd tell him to take a long walk."

"That's what I've done," said Dyana quietly. "And there's an end to it. I won't go through this anymore. I could put up with the publicity and the torture of media exposure and the embarrassment of innuendo and speculation, but I will *not* put up with all the other women. And it is obvious to me that he will not give them up."

A week passed. Chad didn't try to call anymore. He wrote one letter, which Dyana refused to read. She was tired of excuses. All they did was hurt her. When the Crusaders' game came on television, she turned off the power and sat down on the couch with Josie and a good book that couldn't keep her attention.

In about an hour there was a knock on the door.

"Darcy again," she thought, but when she opened the door, it was Chad.

He didn't give her a chance to shut it. Instead he forced his way through, slammed it shut, locked it, and grabbed her as if he wanted to shake her.

"What the hell is going on?" he asked through clenched teeth. "Why won't you talk to me?"

"How can you ask me that?" she wanted to know. "After that little episode with Stacy Carleton after the Bengals game?"

He kissed her hard, ruthlessly, bruising her lips, crushing the breath out of her. "I ought to shake you instead of kissing you," he remarked when he raised his head.

"Chad, you have told me ten thousand times that the other women are just for show. I expected the show would stop, once you said you were committed to me." She tried to twist out of his grasp. "Let go of me and get out of here."

"You must be joking," he said angrily. "I intend to stay here until we have this worked out."

"How many other women have there been, Chad? I've seen dozens over the years." She wouldn't look at him.

"Several," he admitted tersely. He wouldn't let go of her, keeping his left arm behind her back so that she couldn't move, and when she pushed at him, he caught both her wrists tightly with one big hand. "Hell, Dyana, I didn't see you for ten years. I know now that I never, ever quit loving you. I couldn't. But I tried. And did you think I'd spend those years reading great books and contemplating my navel? *You* didn't. There've been other men for you, so why are you so upset that there have been other women for me?"

"I gave up the other men when I decided I love you. You didn't give up the other women."

"Stacy, for your information, had just confided to me that she was about to be married when I kissed her. It was for congratulations and good luck." He did let go of her, then, and ran his fingers through his thick hair with a frustrated gesture. "I can guess the person I should have kissed for luck was the poor sucker she's trapped."

Dyana had her back to him. "What about the cheerleaders, Chad, and all the other women I've seen you with your arm around in the last few weeks? What's going to happen when I'm not around and you need a woman for 'show'?"

Chad touched her arm. "God, Dyana," he said gently, "I had no idea how hurt you were. I thought you were just mad. I'll never physically touch another woman again, unless I'm related to her."

"Don't, please," she said, on the verge of tears. "Just go away and leave me alone."

"I will go away," he said, "because I want to give you the opportunity to think about what I am going to say. I love you, Dyana. You know that. I have never stopped loving you. I want to marry you."

"I can't," she said.

"You love me. I know you do."

The anguish in her heart showed in her eyes. "Yes. So much that it will probably destroy me. But I can't live with the constant insecurity—the exposure and the speculation—and, worst of all, the women. Chad, whatever you say, you like having them fawn over you."

"Remember what I said about not letting all the media hype go to your head? It's the same thing with the women. You like it when they say you're God's gift to females, but you don't take it seriously."

Dyana's disbelief showed on her face.

"Darling, please believe me," Chad said. "It's not me they want. They want the money and the glamour and the fast cars and the big houses and furs and diamonds and introductions to influential people they think I can provide. They aren't interested in me at all. They just pretend to be."

Dyana gave a tinny, bitter, fragile laugh. "That's what you think. Have you looked at yourself? Do you know how desirable you are?"

"I'm glad you think so." He smiled, but above the smile, his eyes were very worried. "It's all artificial, the way I act when I'm around any woman but you. It's a show I put on for the newspapers and the television, so I won't come across as a complete bore. The weekend I spent with you was the first time since I left Rolling Meadows as a boy that I have forgotten completely how I am supposed to act in public and been the man I know I am when the lights are off and the doors are locked and I'm alone." He reached for her hands. "That's the man you've seen, and that's the man you want, Dyana. You will still want me when I'm sixty and paunchy and have to wear reading glasses. And I want you—not any other woman, not ever—and I will still want you when you're sixty and tint your hair and look better than I do because you don't drink beer and you exercise."

He raised her chin and kissed her again, with great tenderness. "I have to go, darling. I have a game day after tomorrow, and I must be there. They need me. And until I can call, please think about what I've told you."

At the door he paused and looked back. "I love you, Dyana. I have loved you most of my life. I started loving you before I put sand in your hair, and I will love you until I die. Think about that."

And he was gone.

She thought about it. She thought about nothing else. It haunted her mind and tortured her emotions. She wanted to believe him, more than anything. Doubtless he had told her what he thought to be the truth. But Dyana thought that the truth was in his actions. How could any man give up all that adulation when he was so accustomed to it? It was like heroin or cocaine—terribly addicting, and destroying what it touched. She had to see that it didn't destroy her.

Susan came over just before the game. Dyana didn't have the television on.

"Aren't you even going to watch?" Susan wanted to know, turning on the television and raising the volume. the pregame show was under way, and as usual, the sportscasters were talking about Chad.

"No," said Dyana simply. "I'm trying to get that out of my mind."

"You are being entirely unreasonable," said Susan, and Dyana thought she heard contempt behind the impatience. "All right, so you don't want him. Turn him over to me. I believe what he says. I don't think he wants another woman, but if I can make him want me, I'm going to do it. He is an outstanding man, morally and emotionally, and you are absolutely crazy to turn down the kind of happiness he can offer you." She went to the door.

"Where are you going?" Dyana asked. She was depressed and wanted Susan's company.

"Frankly I can't stand any more of this. Don't watch the game, if that's what makes you most miserable. I'm going over to Darcy's." And with that parting shot, Susan left.

Dyana sat on the couch, sobbing into Josie's fur. "You're the only one in the whole wide world who loves me," she told the cat unreasonably.

The game impinged only peripherally on her consciousness. Gradually she became aware that the Crusaders were behind, and the commentators were talking about Chad.

"He's not playing nearly as well as he usually does," said one. "Doesn't seem to be able to concentrate on the game."

The other man agreed. "He's made some mistakes that have cost the Crusaders not only yardage but penalties and points as well."

Then Dyana began to watch. Chad was a little late responding to the signals in a couple of plays and moved too fast on another, which cost the Crusaders five yards for being offside. The camera zoomed in for a close-up, and the frustration showed on his face. On the next play he caught a pass but fumbled the ball, and as he was trying to recover, a tackle caught him and knocked him sideways. Before he hit the ground, four more huge men slammed into him. She could see his head snap, see the pain on his face.

When the pile cleared, he didn't get up.

Her heart stopped.

Both coaches and all the referees ran to his side. He was competely motionless on the field. They worked over him for a few minutes, taking off his helmet and examining his eyes. Then one of the men signaled for a stretcher. They lifted him carefully and carried him to an ambulance. The doors shut him away from Dyana's sight.

When Darcy showed up at her door fifteen minutes later, Dyana was packing.

"Chad was right and you were right and Susan was right. I don't care about anything but Chad," Dyana said. "I'm going to California. I'll beat off the damn women with a stick."

Darcy gave her a heartfelt hug. "You're doing the right thing, darling. I'll take care of Josie while you're gone."

"Josie is going with me," said Dyana. "I'm not coming back. The school will have to find another counselor." She smiled tremulously. "Unless he's not all right."

"He'll be all right, Imp. Try not to worry until you get there and find out what's really going on."

It was good advice, but Dyana knew she couldn't follow it.

"Have you made plane reservations?" Darcy asked.

Dyana looked at the ceiling. "Of course not. I forgot. Oh, Darcy—what if I can't get out of here till tomorrow?"

"There are a thousand flights a day going in that direction. We'll get you on one of them," said Darcy decisively. Before she could pick up the phone to dial, it rang.

It was the Crusaders' team manager.

"How is he?" Dyana asked anxiously.

"Looks like a bad concussion. Maybe even worse than that," said the manager. "The doctors won't be able to tell how extensive the damage is for a few hours. He took a pretty bad hit to the neck, as well as the damage to his head. They're doing a CAT scan as soon as he's stabilized."

"Oh, God," said Dyana.

"He's not really fully alert, but he's very restless, and all he can say is to call you to tell you not to worry." The manager paused. "I think you ought to come out here, Miss Kincaid, if you love him."

"I love him," said Dyana. "And I'll be there on the next available flight."

The manager wasn't reassuring. "I think that's a good idea. He needs you here. Have somebody call and we'll meet you at the airport."

Dyana turned to Darcy, in tears. "He's hurt really badly Darce. What am I going to do?"

Darcy was dialing the airlines. "Just love him. That's all you can do. And pray."

While Darcy made the reservations Dyana got the little pink crystal out of its hiding place and put it where it belonged.

The California sun made a strange contrast to the somber face of the man who met Dyana at the airport. Outside the hospital room, a cadre of reporters and television cameras was gathered.

"Miss Kincaid! Miss Kincaid! What do you know? How is Chad doing?"

"I can't tell you that now," she said, shoving her way through the crowd.

"What are you going to do now that you're here?"

She turned around and faced the cameras. "I am going to wait until he gets out of this hospital, and then I am going to take him to Reno and make him marry me." With that she turned and entered Chad's room.

He was awake and smiling, and when the door swung to, he tried to sit up.

"Don't darling," said Dyana, alarmed.

"I'm all right," Chad assured her. "Just a little concussion. I'll be fine in two weeks." He pushed himself up in the bed again. "Give me a kiss."

"Not until you lie back down."

"Bossy," he said, but he put his head down carefully, looking as if the effort to rise had exhausted him.

She bent over him and touched his lips with hers. He put his hand behind her head and held her there for a second, moving his mouth seductively over hers, dipping lightly with his tongue teasing her.

"Stop that! You're a sick man!"

"Giving me orders already?" he said wickedly. "We're not even married yet."

"What makes you think I would want to marry an old, beat-up football player like you?" she asked, sitting on the edge of the bed. "I only came out here to give blood if you needed it."

"Shouldn't lie to the man you love, darling," Chad told her. "I heard you say it with your own two lips."

"When?" she said.

"Kiss me again and I'll tell you."

This time he used both hands, and the kiss lasted longer.

"So how'd you know?" Dyana murmured against his lips.

"Look behind you."

The television was on. The picture on the screen was the hall outside Chad's hospital room, and the reporter to whom she had just talked was analyzing what she'd said, as if it hadn't been perfectly clear.

Dyana kissed Chad again. "You've found me out."

"I love you," said Chad. "Did you know that?"

She regarded him seriously. "I'll never doubt it

again. Oh, Chad, I'm sorry. I've been an idiot."

"Well," he said. "I guess I have, too. But I swear I'll never give you cause to question my fidelity."

"I wouldn't do it, anyway. I've made up my mind. Part of my duty as a wife is to trust in my husband."

"Open the door," said Chad. He looked absurdly happy. "Let's announce our engagement."

AMERICAN FAMILY PUBLISHERS
HAS A WIDE VARIETY OF
EXCELLENT MAGAZINES AT
UNBEATABLE DISCOUNTS.
TO ORDER, WRITE:
AMERICAN FAMILY PUBLISHERS,
MULTI-MILLION DOLLAR
SWEEPSTAKES
P.O. BOX 62000,
TAMPA, FLORIDA 33662